Fargo was so quick that the men hadn't even stopped laughing before his Colt was in his hand. The one whose pistol was on the table made a grab for it, but Fargo put a bullet into the bridge of his nose before he could get it clear of the tabletop.

The other man threw open his robe and pulled his own gun. Fargo let him get it almost level before he shot him in the eye.

Then he whirled around to see that Tom had thrown the woman aside and had his pistol out. He was smiling at Fargo.

"You shouldn't have done that, friend."

"I'm not your friend," Fargo said.

"No, I guess you ain't," Tom said.

He was about to pull the trigger when Fargo shot him. Tom slumped to his knees on the floor, looking up, eyes stunned.

"You son of a bitch," he said.

Fargo didn't bother to answer.

Tom fell forward on his face. His left leg twitched once, and the toe of his boot kicked the dirt floor. Then he was still.

GUNS AND BAD MEN

THE
TRAILSMAN
#255

MONTANA
MADMEN

by

Jon Sharpe

A SIGNET BOOK

SIGNET
Published by New American Library, a division of
Penguin Putnam Inc., 375 Hudson Street,
New York, New York 10014, U.S.A.
Penguin Books Ltd, 80 Strand,
London WC2R 0RL, England
Penguin Books Australia Ltd, 250 Camberwell Road,
Camberwell, Victoria 3124, Australia
Penguin Books Canada Ltd, 10 Alcorn Avenue,
Toronto, Ontario, Canada M4V 3B2
Penguin Books (N.Z.) Ltd, Cnr Rosedale and Airborne Roads,
Albany, Auckland 1310, New Zealand

Penguin Books Ltd, Registered Offices:
Harmondsworth, Middlesex, England

First published by Signet, an imprint of New American Library,
a division of Penguin Putnam Inc.

First Printing, January 2003
10 9 8 7 6 5 4 3 2 1

The first chapter of this title originally appeared in *Nebraska Gunrunners*,
the two hundred fifty-fourth volume in this series.

🅙 REGISTERED TRADEMARK—MARCA REGISTRADA

Printed in the United States of America

PUBLISHER'S NOTE
This is a work of fiction. Names, characters, places, and incidents either are
the product of the author's imagination or are used fictitiously, and any
resemblance to actual persons, living or dead, business establishments, events,
or locales is entirely coincidental.

The Trailsman

Beginnings . . . they bend the tree and they mark the man. Skye Fargo was born when he was eighteen. Terror was his midwife, vengeance his first cry. Killing spawned Skye Fargo, ruthless, cold-blooded murder. Out of the acrid smoke of gunpowder still hanging in the air, he rose, cried out a promise never forgotten.

The Trailsman they began to call him all across the West: searcher, scout, hunter, the man who could see where others only looked, his skills for hire but not his soul, the man who lived each day to the fullest, yet trailed each tomorrow. Skye Fargo, the Trailsman, the seeker who could take the wildness of a land and the wanting of a woman and make them his own.

Bitterroot Valley, 1862—
There's gold in Devil's Creek, and madness
in the marshal.

1

The trading post west of Fort Sheridan wasn't any different from a lot of those that Skye Fargo had seen—not much more than a ramshackle hut, dark and dirty, smoky and smelly, with a few tables and a makeshift bar. Anybody could turn up in a place like that, from the best to the worst, but it was usually the worst. The man should have known that, Fargo thought. He should never have brought the woman there.

But it was none of Fargo's business, or so he told himself. He had other things on his mind, but even so, his lake-blue eyes turned icy when he heard the comments of the men at the table in the darkest corner of the room.

There were three of them, and they wore heavy buffalo robes, though it was too far into the spring for such things. They smelled worse than the dead animals they'd taken the hides from, and their faces were hidden by heavy beards. Their voices were coarse and loud, as if they'd been drinking for quite a spell.

The couple could hear them, too, probably better than Fargo could. It was plain that they were trying to ignore the roughnecks, but Fargo figured that it would soon be impossible.

He was right. It wasn't long before one of the men stood up and said something that made the woman avert her face. The man and his friends laughed, and he walked over to the table where the woman sat, his heavy robe dragging on the hard-packed dirt floor. He wore a beaver hat that had seen better days. Some of the fur was missing, and what remained was stained and greasy.

The trading post owner, a short, skinny man named

Barsett, was behind the rickety bar, and he started to reach for something that Fargo couldn't see, but one of the men still sitting at the table reached inside his robe and brought out a heavy Navy Colt and laid it on the tabletop with an audible thump. Barsett looked up, and the man shook his head at him. Barsett smiled a weaselly smile and walked to the far end of the room, where he pushed aside a dirty cloth that served as a curtain and went out. It was clear that he wasn't going to interfere with whatever happened.

The man with the pistol looked over at Fargo and gave him a gap-toothed grin as if to say that the fun was about to begin. The grin was not, however, an invitation for Fargo to join in. It was a clear sign that Fargo wasn't to do anything at all, other than to stay right where he was and ignore what was going on. Fargo took a drink of his sorry-tasting whiskey and didn't say a word.

The big man had reached the woman's table by then, and he was looking down at the man Fargo assumed was her husband, who started to stand up.

"Don't, Moses," the woman said, but she was too late because Moses was already halfway out of his chair.

The big man put out a ham-sized hand and shoved Moses back into the chair so hard that it wobbled backward and nearly overturned.

"You just be quiet and keep your seat, Moses," the big man said, "while I talk to this pretty little lady here."

She was pretty, all right, Fargo thought, or at least what he could see of her was. She had night-black hair and delicate features, with a wide mouth and big black eyes. She was wearing a man's heavy shirt that effectively covered any other charms she might have above the waist, and her lower body was hidden by the table where she sat.

She looked up at the man and said, "Leave us alone. Please. Just go away."

He grinned down at her and said, "You can call me Tom, and I ain't goin' away. I like the way you say please. I think I'd like to hear you say it again."

"Please," she said, looking down at the table.

The big man looked around at his friends and said, "Ain't that just about the sweetest thing you ever heard?"

He laughed, and one of them said, "It sure is, Tom. Tell her to say it one more time."

"You heard him," Tom told her. "Say it again."

The woman, who was still looking down at the table, opened her mouth, but this time no sound came out.

"Say it," Tom told her, his voice rough with anger.

"Leave her alone," Moses said.

"No, Moses," his wife said, but again she was too late. Moses was already clawing awkwardly for the pistol he wore at his side.

Tom didn't give him a chance to get it. He grabbed Moses by the collar and jerked him out of the chair.

"Don't ever try to pull a gun on me, son," Tom said.

He threw Moses to the floor and nodded toward the table in the corner. The man who had laid the pistol on the table picked it up and fired twice. The first bullet struck Moses in the center of the chest. He was probably already dead when the second bullet took off the side of his jaw.

The sound of the shots echoed in the room, and for a while all Fargo could hear was the ringing in his ears. He smelled the bitter powder smoke and wondered again what a man like Moses had been doing in the trading post and why he'd brought the woman there.

Tom was saying something to the woman, but he kept his voice low, and Fargo couldn't quite hear what it was. The woman probably couldn't either, as she stared in shocked silence at the dead man, her eyes wide in disbelief.

The two men at the other table were laughing. Fargo couldn't hear them, either, but he saw their wide mouths and squinted eyes as the shooter dropped his Colt back on the table.

Fargo looked back at the woman. She eased out of the chair and onto the floor as if she wanted to cradle the dead man's head in her arms but was too sickened by the blood and tissue to do it.

Tom reached for her, but she struck away his hand. She was spirited, and that seemed to make him angry. He reached again, grabbing a fistful of her shirt. She tried to pull away, but he drew her up from the floor and to him. When he had her standing, he opened the buffalo robe with one hand and hugged her against his chest with the other. He pressed his bearded face to hers for a kiss. She turned her head aside, but that didn't bother Tom. He nuzzled her neck like a horse eating oats while she struggled to break his grip.

Fargo told himself that it wasn't his problem. He had things to do, and he couldn't let himself be distracted by the troubles of other people. They should have known better than to get themselves in such a bad fix, and if they had blundered into a bad situation, well, they deserved what had happened. Besides, Fargo had learned the hard way that nearly every time he got mixed into somebody else's business, it led to trouble for him. And he didn't need any more trouble right at the moment.

He told himself all that, but it wasn't helping much. He could see the two men laughing at their table, licking their lips in anticipation of what was to come. Fargo had a good idea of what that would be. As soon as Tom had his way with the woman, he'd give her to them, and by the time they were done with her, there wouldn't be much more left of her than there was of those buffalo the men had skinned for their robes.

Fargo sighed. He couldn't see himself letting that happen, even though he was sure he'd regret stepping in. He stood up and faced the men at the table. He was so quick that they hadn't even stopped laughing before his Colt was in his hand. The one whose pistol was on the table made a grab for it, but Fargo put a bullet in the bridge of his nose before he could get it clear of the tabletop.

The other man threw open his robe and pulled his own gun. Fargo let him get it almost level before he shot him in the right eye.

Fargo then whirled around to see that Tom had thrown the woman aside. She had landed on the table, knocking it over, and it had fallen on top of her after she hit the dirt floor.

Tom had his pistol out, and he was smiling at Fargo.

"You shouldn't have done that, friend."

"I'm not your friend," Fargo said.

"No, I guess you ain't," Tom said.

He was about to pull the trigger when Fargo shot him the first time. Dust puffed out of the robe where the bullet struck, and Tom looked surprised. He looked even more surprised when Fargo shot him again, the bullet striking him in almost the same place the first one had. He slumped to his knees on the floor, looking up at Fargo, his eyes stunned. His beaver had fallen off and rolled to the side.

4

"You son of a bitch," he said.

Fargo didn't bother to answer. He just waited. He didn't have to wait long.

Tom fell forward on his face. His left leg twitched once, and the toe of his boot kicked the dirt floor. Then he was still.

The room was full of acrid smoke. Now that the shooting was over, Fargo waved it away from his face. Then he went back to his table and had a drink from his whiskey glass.

The woman stirred and looked around, wide-eyed. Fargo put the whiskey glass down on the table. He went over to the woman and helped her to her feet. What with all the shooting in the enclosed space, it would be a while before either of them could hear much of anything, so he led her outside and leaned her against the wall. Her shoulders shook as sobs racked her body, and Fargo left her to her grief.

It was a warm spring day. There wasn't a cloud to be seen in the high blue sky, and the grass around the trading post waved in the breeze. Fargo stood and let the sun warm him.

After ten or fifteen minutes, he started hearing sounds again, mainly the sobs of the woman. He was surprised she hadn't stopped crying by now.

He left her where she was and went back inside. The weasel-faced Barsett was standing over Tom's body, looking like he was about to cry, too. He wasn't grieving, however. He was just angry.

Barsett turned to Fargo and said, "You son of a bitch. What are you gonna do about all this?"

"Not one damn thing," Fargo told him. "This is your fault, Barsett. If you'd pulled your shotgun out from under the bar before it started, it never would've happened."

"Goddammit, I'll set the law on you."

"The hell you will. You know what they'd have done to that woman. You probably would've helped, you little bastard."

Barsett opened his mouth, then looked at the face of the big man in the buckskins and closed it.

"That's better," Fargo told him. "What you'd better do is bury those three and forget about anything ever happening here. It won't be the first time."

Barsett didn't deny the accusation. Finally he said, "Who's gonna pay me for the damages?"

"I don't see any damages," Fargo said. "Just four dead men. You can keep the robes off those three, and you can take whatever else they have on them for your trouble."

Barsett thought it over while Fargo watched him. It didn't matter to Fargo what the man decided. Fargo was leaving, no matter what.

"I guess that's fair," Barsett said after a few seconds. He seemed about to say something else, but he caught himself and clamped his mouth shut.

"I know what you're thinking," Fargo said. "You can have their horses, too. I don't care."

Barsett rubbed his hands together in satisfaction.

"What about the other fella?" he asked.

"His things go with the woman."

"Yeah, I figured. What about her?"

"You can't have her," Fargo said.

"A man like you don't need a woman taggin' along with him. What're you gonna do with her?"

It was a good question, and Fargo hadn't really thought that far ahead. He said, "We'll have to see about that."

He left Barsett standing there and went outside. The woman was still right where he'd left her, but she'd stopped crying. Fargo looked at her appraisingly.

"They killed Moses," she said, meeting his gaze.

"They did that," Fargo agreed. "He should've known better than to bring a woman like you out here with nobody to back him up. You should've been with a party, or had a guide."

Fargo had taken people all over the west. He knew about guides, and he knew about all the dangers that people could encounter, from Indians to animals to weather. And men like Tom and his partners.

"We couldn't afford a guide," the woman said.

Fargo looked back at the door of the trading post as if he could see what was inside it.

"I know what you're thinking," the woman said. "If we'd spent the money, Moses would be alive now. But we didn't have the money to spend even if we'd wanted to. That's why we were going west. My brother's here. He says there's gold. Moses was going to try his luck."

6

Fargo looked the woman over. He'd been right about her looks, and now that he could see more of her, he knew that her body lived up to the promise of her face. She was wearing denim pants that fit tightly around her well-rounded rump, and her legs were long and slim.

"Where were you headed?" he asked.

"Devil's Creek. Did you ever hear of it?"

"I've heard of it," Fargo said.

"I'll never get there now. My God. What am I going to do?"

"I can take you there," Fargo told her.

"What?" She looked at him quizzically. "Why would you do that?"

"Because," Fargo said, "I'm headed there myself."

The woman's name was Ruth, and she didn't want to spend the night at the trading post.

"I want to get as far away from here as we can," she said. "But I can't leave until Moses is buried."

Fargo hadn't planned to stay around for that part of things, but he helped Barsett drag the bodies out behind the building, and then he helped dig Moses's grave. Ruth insisted on saying a few words over her husband before they covered him over, and then she started crying again. While she was getting over it, Barsett went back inside, and Fargo got the horses ready to go. He mounted up on the big Ovaro and rode back to the grave, leading Ruth's horse and her husband's.

"You ready?" he asked.

She looked at him and said that she was. She mounted her own horse with practiced ease and said, "Let's go."

They rode away, and neither one of them looked back.

2

After they'd ridden a few miles, Ruth started talking. She explained that she and her husband had come from Kansas. Moses had failed as a farmer and then failed as a businessman. He'd even tried a little school teaching and failed at that.

"So he decided we needed a fresh start," Ruth said. "He thought that if we could find gold, things would be all right."

Most men who thought along those lines went out on their own, Fargo thought. They didn't take their wives with them. He said as much to Ruth.

"I know, but Moses didn't like to be alone. He needed somebody with him."

Fargo had known men like that. It was as if they'd never quite figured out how to get along in life, and they needed someone else to take care of them. The western territories were no place for men like that, as most of them had found out the hard way.

Ruth went on to say that she and Moses had gotten as far as Denver without too much difficulty, but after that, things had grown worse. Moses didn't really know anything about the country or about how to travel in it. They'd more or less wandered from one place to another, and while Moses kept promising Ruth that they'd get to the Bitterroot Valley and start getting rich on a gold claim, they didn't seem to be making a lot of progress.

"He said he just knew that things were going to work out," Ruth said. "He told me that we'd be rich." She shook her head. "I guess he was wrong."

"I guess he was," Fargo said.

"Is that why you're going to Devil's Creek?" Ruth asked. "To get rich?"

"No," Fargo said.

"Why, then?"

"I have my reasons," Fargo said.

He wasn't going to talk about them with Ruth, however. What he was going to do in the territory was none of her business.

They were silent for a time, and then she said, "I can tell you're not like Moses. You know your way around out here."

It was true. Fargo was a trailsman, and he had traveled over the whole of the west. He had spent some time down Texas way and seen the Gulf waters roll onto Galveston island. He had seen the Tetons in the Yellowstone, and he'd seen the silver mines of Nevada. When you got right down to it, there wasn't much he'd missed.

But being a trailsman meant more than just traveling around and being able to find his way where others couldn't. It meant that he had developed a kind of sensitivity to his surroundings, that he could read the signs that were visible and the ones that weren't. He could respond to the unseen, the unheard, the unsaid. It was a special kind of receptiveness that most white men never even understood, much less cultivated, but Fargo had it. And it was warning him now, warning him that there was more to the woman Ruth than met the eye and that there was danger ahead of him and danger behind him.

He knew about the danger in front of him. That was why he was headed to Devil's Creek in the first place. But the danger behind was something different, something that he was keen to even though he couldn't name it. It caused a prickling at the base of his neck, but he didn't worry about it. He knew he'd meet it soon enough.

They camped that evening by a small stream. It became clear that Ruth had spent time in the open before. She knew how to build a fire, and she set about it while Fargo tried his hand at fishing. He caught a couple of small trout and cleaned them beside the stream, tossing the offal on the ground for the scavengers that would show up soon after nightfall.

Ruth fried the trout in a black iron skillet, and Fargo had to admit that they tasted as good as if he'd done the job himself. He said so.

"Thank you," Ruth said. "I've always prided myself on my cooking."

When they were finished, she took the skillet down to the stream and scoured it out with sand from the bank. Dusk was gathering, and Fargo suggested that they might as well get out their bedrolls.

Ruth was careful to carry her things quite a distance from Fargo. She chose a spot under a large tree. Fargo preferred to be in the open.

It grew dark. Fargo settled his head back and looked up at the stars that glittered like fiery pinpricks in the black sky. A three-quarter moon, pale as ice, rose slowly and cast dark shadows around the trees. Fargo thought he heard Ruth crying just as he drifted off to sleep.

He didn't know what woke him, but he was instantly alert, his pistol in his hand. He saw Ruth's silhouette in the moonlight a few yards off.

"What's the matter?" Fargo asked.

"I didn't mean to bother you," she said. "I couldn't sleep, and I thought a walk around might help."

"You don't want to be walking around out here," Fargo told her. "You never know what you might run into."

She shuddered. "Could anything be worse than what I've already encountered?"

Fargo smiled ruefully, though he knew she couldn't see.

"You've got a lot to learn about this place," he said. "There are a lot worse things here than Tom."

Ruth walked closer.

"You know what he wanted," she said.

Fargo said that he knew, all right.

"Do you want it, too?"

"What the hell kind of a question is that?" Fargo asked.

"It's just a question. I've never quite been able to figure out why men act the way they do. Moses never did. He just never seemed interested." She paused. "Well, hardly ever. And when he did, it was never very exciting."

"You think it would've been exciting with Tom?" Fargo asked.

Ruth moved closer still. She was standing so close now that Fargo could have reached out and touched her leg.

"I don't think it would have been exciting," she said. "I think it would have been painful and sad."

Fargo wasn't sure she was right about the sad part, but she was damn sure right about the painful, at least as far as she was concerned. It wouldn't have hurt Tom much.

"I wonder what it would be like with you," she said.

Fargo didn't answer because he didn't know what to make of her. Here she was, after all her crying and her husband not dead more than a few hours, practically offering herself to him. One thing was for sure, though. It was an offer he wasn't going to turn down, not if she really meant it.

"You could always find out," he said.

"I guess I could, at that."

Ruth knelt down beside him and looked into his eyes, smiling almost shyly. Then she put her hands to the sides of his head and put her mouth on his. The kiss started off awkwardly, but it soon caught fire. Ruth's tongue darted into Fargo's mouth, tangled with his, then withdrew. She leaned away from him, breathing heavily.

"Moses never kissed me like that."

Fargo could tell. He was thinking that there must have been a lot Moses hadn't done, or at least hadn't done right. Fargo could do it right, and he was glad that Ruth was curious enough to find out what she'd been missing. Most women would have been afraid. He reached out and started to undo the buttons of her shirt.

He didn't work fast enough, and Ruth moved his hand away. Fargo was surprised at the speed with which she got her clothing off. When she stood before him naked in the moonlight, she said, "Do I look all right?"

Fargo admired the creamy hills of her breasts, her slim calves, her tight, flat belly, the fleecy hair at the juncture of her legs.

"You look better than that," he said. "Didn't Moses ever tell you?"

"Moses never saw me like this," she said. "He didn't want to. He thought it wasn't right for a woman to show her nakedness to a man."

Now Moses would never know what he had missed,

11

Fargo thought. He must have been as crazy as a donkey grazing in a patch of loco weed.

She ran her hands tentatively over her breasts and shivered. Fargo shivered a little, too, and started shucking off his clothing. Soon he was as naked as she was, his pole jutting out in front of him.

"My God," Ruth said. She reached out a hand and touched him gingerly. "Moses never looked like that!"

Fargo was beginning to feel truly sorry for Moses, who was never going to know what he'd missed out on by being such a pantywaist. He stepped close to Ruth, pressing the length of his shaft up against her belly and letting her feel its heat. Her soft breasts flattened against his chest, and their hard tips felt like tiny hot coals.

They kissed again, and this time when they drew apart, Ruth was shaking as if she had a chill, and her skin was hot to the touch.

"I feel feverish," she said.

"It's not fever," Fargo said. "And if it is, I have the cure for it."

They lay down side by side on the grass, and Fargo let his hands roam over her body, feeling the fullness of the ripe breasts and the rise of her hips. His fingers lingered in the tangled curls of Ruth's pubic hair, and she moaned softly as he ran his hand between her legs and down her inner thighs.

She opened her legs and let him explore her more fully. His finger found her nether lips and stroked them for a moment before he slipped it between them. When he did that, Ruth cried out.

"Oh! Oh!"

So that was something else Moses had never done, Fargo thought. He stopped the motion of his finger.

"Oh, don't stop!" Ruth said. "Please! Please!"

He continued to caress her, and soon her hips were bucking against his hand. He pressed down on her pubic mound and held his finger still while she did the work, rocking herself in ecstasy. She raised her hips high, and almost without volition his finger slipped inside her. She was so wet and slickery that it went in right past the second knuckle.

"Ah! Ah!" Ruth cried, and thrust at him.

Fargo moved his hand away and looked at her. She grew calmer and reached for his stiff pole.

"Put it in me now," she said. "I want to feel it in me."

Fargo was more than ready to oblige, up to a point. He settled himself between her legs, but he didn't insert himself. Instead he let the hairs around her sweet spot tickle the sensitive tip of his tool. Then he slid inside just enough to bring her excitement to a new level.

"Oh, sweet Jesus!" Ruth said. "Now, Fargo! Please! I have to have it now!"

Fargo didn't see any reason not to give her what she was asking for. He wanted it as much as she did, if not more. He slipped into her as easily as if she had been oiled, all the way to the bottom of his root. For a second or two they remained like that, completely motionless, Fargo buried in her so far that their pubic hair tangled. Then Ruth began to moan deep in her throat. Suddenly she threw her legs around Fargo's back and locked her ankles together. She thrashed beneath him as if she were in her death throes, and Fargo had to struggle to match her movements. In moments, however, they were working together as if they'd been doing it for years, and Ruth became even more frenzied.

Then all at once she stopped moving completely. She lay still as death, and a small noise began to come from somewhere deep inside her. It grew louder and louder. She dug her nails into Fargo's back and began to rock under him, slowly at first and then faster and faster. Finally a loud cry burst from her.

"Now! Now! Now!"

Fargo could hold back no longer. He pushed his hips against her with each shuttering climax, forcing himself deeper and deeper into her until they both came to a stop, exhausted.

They lay without speaking for a long while. Then Fargo said, "Was it exciting?"

"My God, yes. Yes. I didn't know it could be like that. It was never like that with Moses. Never. Will it ever be like that again?"

"Could be," Fargo said.

"Good. When? How soon?"

"Well, I figure it'll be at least a few minutes," Fargo said. "You think you can wait that long?"

Ruth laughed. It was a sound of pure joy.

"I'll try," she said.

* * *

The next morning, Fargo wasn't sure he was going to be able to walk, much less ride a horse. For the rest of the previous night, Ruth had been like a woman possessed. He had never met one more insistent or demanding. Not that he minded. It had been quite an experience for both of them. Ruth had never known real sex before, and Fargo had enjoyed teaching her what it was all about. He wondered if she would ever cry for Moses again. Somehow he didn't think so.

3

They reached Devil's Creek after a week's slow traveling.
After the first night, Fargo hadn't been in any hurry. His
business there wasn't urgent.

The town was located in the Bitterroot Valley, and the
creek from which the town took its name flowed into the
Bitterroot River. To the west of the town were the Bitterroot Mountains, rising dark against the blue sky. Though
it was spring in the valley, there was still snow high on the
mountains, and it gleamed white in the sun.

Fargo had been to the valley before. Because of the
warm winds from the ocean that came in over the mountains, Bitterroot Valley was more temperate than a lot of
the rest of the state, even in the winter, and things grew
better there. The blue sky curved over the valley like a
bowl. Red and blue wildflowers bloomed, and the leaves
on the cottonwood trees were green. Pine needles glistened.
Birds sang in the tree branches. A small herd of white-
tailed deer stood near a stand of poplar trees, silently
watching Fargo and Ruth. Then one of them flipped up a
tail, and they all vanished into the trees as if they'd never
existed. A person who didn't know better might think he'd
stumbled onto some kind of earthly paradise.

Fargo knew better, but he didn't say anything about it
to Ruth. They sat on their horses, looking down at the little
town, and he said, "What's your brother's name?"

"Samuel. Like the prophet in the Bible. Our parents
liked those kinds of names. Do you think we can find him?"

"We shouldn't have much trouble," Fargo said. "Everybody knows everybody else in a little place like Devil's
Creek."

They rode on down into the town. It was like many other towns that had sprung up when there was a rumor of gold: filled with flapping tents and hastily assembled buildings so new that Fargo could smell the green lumber. Most of the buildings were so rickety that they wouldn't stand up to a halfway strong wind. It was no surprise to Fargo that the two most substantial structures in the whole place were the jail and the gallows.

The rutted streets were bustling with people and wagons. There was a smell of horse manure and mud in the air. A few dogs barked along behind one of the wagons, and three women lounging outside one of the tents laughed at them.

"Those women aren't decent," Ruth said.

Fargo wasn't quite sure of her meaning. She might have been referring to their posture or their dress, or both. One of the women, a blonde, sat with her foot resting in her chair. She had a ragged scar like a piece of dirty string on the side of her face. Another woman, this one a brassy redhead, was wearing only a thin robe that did little to conceal what was underneath it. She smiled and waved at Fargo, tossing her long red hair.

"Whores," Fargo said. "They'll probably take more gold out of this town than any miner ever will."

Ruth looked shocked, as if she hadn't known such women existed.

"They should be ashamed of themselves," she said. She paused. Then her face turned red and she laughed. "Not that I'm any better than they are."

Fargo grinned. "I'd say you were probably a whole lot better."

Ruth's face turned even redder, and Fargo figured she was thinking about their days on the trail, or rather their nights. Ruth had proved that the first night was no accident. It was as if she'd been looking for something her whole life and had finally found it. Fargo had been hard-pressed to keep up with her.

"There's something I didn't tell you about Samuel," she said.

"What's that?" Fargo asked.

"He's a preacher."

Fargo had experience with all kinds of women, all over the west. But about the only thing he'd really learned about them was that he would never be able to figure them out. They would always be able to surprise him in one way or another. He'd thought Ruth's surprise had been her avid appetite for sex, but it turned out that she had another revelation for him.

"He and Moses were best friends," Ruth said. "Sometimes I think Moses should have been a preacher, too."

Fargo said, "Samuel should be pretty easy to find if he's a preacher."

"Why don't we ask somebody?"

Fargo looked around. Some of the men on the street were giving Ruth the eye, and some were looking at Fargo as if trying to figure out what he was doing there and why he was with a woman. Fargo didn't recognize any of them.

"I'm looking for a friend," he said to Ruth.

"I'd forgotten you told me you were coming here. But you never told me the reason."

"That's right," Fargo said. "Let's stop at that saloon."

The saloon, while not as solid as the jail, was one of the better built places in town. There was a sign that said it was the Trail's End.

Fargo slid off the Ovaro and flipped the reins around the hitch rail. He told Ruth to wait for him and went inside.

It was nearly noon, but the saloon was already full of men who were drinking and playing cards. The light was bad, and Fargo blinked to let his eyes adjust. Then he looked around. At one of the tables near the back of the room there was a small man wearing a battered hat. He had a bushy gray beard as tangled as a briar thicket, and he was talking loudly to the others around the table as he dealt from a greasy deck of cards.

"Ante up, gents. This is the game to separate the men from the boys. It'll grow hair on your chests and put blood in your eye. Remember what they say: Think long and you'll think wrong. Just relax and enjoy it and let old Wiley Rawlings take your money."

Fargo walked over to the table and looked at old Wiley's hand. He was holding a pair of deuces, a seven, a five, and a king. When it came his turn to bet, he raised the pot.

"Big money talks and bullshit walks. Old Wiley's raisin' your sorry asses."

One man dropped out, and Wiley said, "Cards to the

17

gamblers, cards to the gamblers. How many do you want?"

He dealt out the numbers that were called for and took three himself. He got another duece.

"Old Wiley's going to kick your asses," he said when he raised the pot again. "You boys won't even know what hit you."

The other men more or less ignored him, and Fargo could tell that he wasn't fooling any of them. They'd probably played with him before, more than once. In the end, he was beaten by three kings.

"Goddammit! I just knew I was gonna take that hand," he said. "Well, you know what they say: Next time's the charm. Whose deal?"

"Hey, Wiley," Fargo said.

Wiley turned around and saw Fargo. He turned back to the table and said, "This is your lucky day, boys. You'll have to deal me out, and I won't be able to take any more of your money."

The players didn't look as if they felt lucky. It was more like they were sorry to see Wiley go. He pushed his chair back and stood up to his full height, which was about five feet, five inches. His bright eyes glittered like mica in the tangle of beard that covered his face.

"Good to see you, Fargo," he said. "I wasn't sure you'd come."

"I'm here, though. Where can we go to talk?"

"I got a place. We can go there."

"There's something I need to take care of first. You know a preacher named Samuel?"

"Goddammed right. Ever'body knows him. He's here tryin' to save souls, but it don't do him much good. There's not another person in this town except him that wouldn't sell out to old Splitfoot in five seconds for a pan of gold from the creek. Well, that's not countin' me. I'm not on the devil's side, nosirree."

Fargo laughed. "When did you change over?"

"Don't you go be makin' fun of old Wiley, now."

Fargo wasn't sure exactly how old Wiley was. He was so dried up and scrawny, and his beard was so gray, that it was hard to tell. All Fargo knew for sure was that Wiley had been around for a long time, had traveled far and seen a lot. He was the one who'd gotten the word to Fargo about Billy Banks.

"I need to see Samuel before we talk," Fargo said. "I've got his sister with me."

Wiley peered up at him. "You manage to get yourself a payin' customer to make the trip with you?"

"That's not exactly the way it happened. Come on and show me where this preacher stays."

"You don't have to ask old Wiley twice. Follow me."

They went outside, where Ruth was waiting on her horse. Wiley was taken with her from the first.

"You told me you had a woman with you," he said so that Ruth could hear, "but you didn't tell me she was an angel. I'm not surprised that her brother's a preacher man. Livin' around a woman like that'd be enough to convert old Scratch himself."

Ruth smiled at him and said, "Who's your flattering friend, Mr. Fargo?"

Fargo told her, and Wiley hopped off the boardwalk and went over to her horse. He reached up and took her right hand with his own, lifting his hat off his head with his left to expose a thick snarl of gray hair.

"I'm mighty pleased to meet you," he said. "I'm gonna take you to your brother, and a fine man he is, too, savin' sinners and drivin' out the devil."

"You can ride our spare horse," Fargo said, and Wiley jumped up on the unsaddled animal's back as readily as a ten-year-old Indian boy.

"Come on along," he said, "and I'll show you the church."

The church was at the opposite end of the town from where Fargo and Ruth had ridden in. It was built of raw logs with the bark still on, and there was only one big room. It hadn't been there the last time Fargo had been in Devil's Creek.

"Samuel came in and took a hold right off," Wiley said as they approached the church. "Built this here church himself, with the help of a few Christians, me included."

Fargo figured Wiley was stretching things a little bit, both the part about being a Christian and the part about helping, probably to make himself sound good to Ruth. But you could never tell about Wiley. He might even have been telling the truth.

"Hello, the church," Wiley sang out as they rode up.

A tall man came outside. His resemblance to Ruth was obvious. He had the same dark hair and eyes. He wore rough work clothes, and the shirt was a little too short for his long arms, so that his thick, knobby wrists protruded from the sleeves. He shaded his eyes with a wide, hard hand and looked to see who was there.

"Ruth?" he said. "Is that you, Ruth?"

She slid off her mount and ran to him. "Samuel!" she said, wrapping her arms around him. He swung her up, laughing.

"I was beginning to think you were never going to get here," he said when he put her down. He looked toward the two men on horseback. "Where's Moses?"

"He's dead," Ruth said. "He was killed in a fight at a trading post. The man in buckskins is Mr. Fargo. He was kind enough to bring me here."

"Dead?" Samuel said. "A fight? That doesn't sound like Moses."

"Some men were trying to hurt me. He stood up to them."

Samuel looked at her as if to say that didn't sound like Moses, either.

"It would have been worse if Mr. Fargo hadn't stepped in," Ruth said. She explained about Tom and the others. "And don't worry about Moses. We buried him proper. I said the words myself."

"It's just hard for me to believe," Samuel said. A dark cloud passed over his face. He gave Fargo a suspicious look. "I can't imagine Moses being dead. He wasn't a violent man."

"Fargo is, though," Wiley said. "If he was mixed in it, you can bet there's some others that're dead, too."

"I don't approve of violence," Samuel said in a way that sounded a little too pious to Fargo. "But I do know there are times when it's necessary. Even our Lord lost his temper once, and drove the money changers from the temple. Sometimes there are outrageous situations that have to be corrected. Whatever you did, Mr. Fargo, I'm sure you were in the right."

Fargo nodded, not really caring just what Samuel thought. Samuel hadn't been there. Fargo had. And there was something about the man that Fargo didn't much like.

Samuel went on. "The only problem now is what to do with Ruth. I don't think she's cut out to be a miner."

"No," she said. "But I can work. I can cook and sew. The men here must need someone to do work like that."

"They do," Samuel said with an odd look in his eyes, "but they don't always know how to treat a woman, especially a single woman."

Fargo thought Samuel was probably thinking of the whores, who were about the only single women making a living in Devil's Creek.

"There must be a few miners with wives," Fargo said. "Some of them might even be members of your church."

Samuel smiled. "Well, of course you're right. Ruth can live with one of those families, and she might even learn to like it here. It will be a chance to start again. Why don't you all come inside, and we can talk it over."

"Me and Fargo's got other things to discuss," Wiley said. "Much as we'd like to stay, we got to move on."

Fargo didn't like for others to speak for him, but Wiley was right. Besides, he didn't have any claims on Ruth and didn't want any. It was time for her to begin making her own decisions.

"All I own is those two horses and what they're carrying," Ruth said. "I won't be much trouble to anybody, and I'm sure I can earn a living."

"We'll see," Samuel told her. "I thank you for your help, Mr. Fargo. Mr. Rawlings."

"No trouble a'tall," Wiley said.

He jumped down from the horse and stepped up to the big Ovaro. Fargo reached down a hand and pulled him up behind him.

"Thank you," Ruth said, walking over to Fargo and smiling up at him. "For everything."

Fargo, who knew exactly what she meant, said, "It was my pleasure, ma'am."

"Maybe we'll meet again," she said.

"Maybe," Fargo said, but he didn't really think so.

4

Billy Banks was buried in a little cemetery that was a little way into the foothills on the way to Wiley's place. Wiley had thought that they should stop by Billy's grave and pay their respects, and Fargo had agreed. The place was mostly raw ground enclosed by a knee-high fence, and it seemed to Fargo that there were too many graves for a town as small and as new as Devil's Creek.

"That's 'cause most of the folks here got themselves hung," Wiley said when Fargo mentioned it. "Lattner's been here a year, and he's hung fifteen men. That's more'n one a month, in case you can't do the 'rithmetic."

"And he always has a good reason?" Fargo asked.

"Good enough for him. Good enough for the town, too, I guess, or most of it."

They were standing by Billy's grave. The raw earth atop it was almost level with the rest of the ground and had a few weeds growing in it. The marker was nothing more than a board with Billy's name and his death date scratched on it. The wind blew and stirred the weeds.

"Not good enough for you, though," Fargo said.

"Nope, and not good enough for you, either, else you wouldn't be here."

Fargo wasn't so sure about that. He said, "Billy was a good man, and he died too young. Let's go."

When they were outside the fence, Wiley closed the gate. They went on their way without looking back.

Wiley Rawlings's place was nothing more than a small canvas tent pitched in some trees in the Sapphire foothills. There wasn't room in it for two men, but Fargo didn't mind that. He'd spent a big part of his life outdoors, and he'd be just as glad to sleep there again.

"Sorry I can't offer you any accommodations," Wiley said. "There ain't a hell of a lot of rooms to let in Devil's Creek right at the moment, what with ever'body comin' in from all over to find gold."

"You think any of them will find it?"

"Some of 'em already have. They're pannin' it out of the creek, a little at a time. And there's plenty of 'em looking for a vein. If they ever find that, there'll be so many people here that you won't be able to stir 'em with a stick. You want some coffee?"

"Never mind that," Fargo said. "Just tell me about Billy Banks."

"It's kind of a long story," Wiley said. "Don't you want to get something to eat first?"

"I've waited this long to hear it. I guess a little longer wouldn't hurt. Where can we eat?"

"You buyin'?"

"How much did you lose at that poker table?"

"Never you mind about that. Old Wiley can take care of himself. I'm doin' just fine, and don't even own a gold pan. If you don't want to buy me something to eat, all you got to do is say so."

"I'll buy," Fargo said.

They wound up at a big tent with a small sign out front telling the world that it was Annie's Place, where they ate tough steak and lumpy gray potatoes. While they were eating, Wiley told Fargo about Billy Banks, who by that time had been dead for three months.

"I sent word for you as soon as they killed him," Wiley said. "But I knew you wouldn't get it for a good while."

Since Fargo was never in one place for very long, sometimes messages took their time reaching him. There probably wasn't anything he could've done for Billy anyhow, but he was curious to see how he'd managed to get himself hanged.

Fargo's first trip to the Bitterroot Valley had been made with Billy. They'd brought in a party of men who were going to settle there, and Billy had been so taken with the place that he decided to stay. It had apparently been a bad decision.

"I knew you'd want to know about it," Wiley said. "'Cause when a man's partner gets killed, he oughta do something about it."

"He wasn't my partner," Fargo said.

"Well, you rode together, so it comes down to the same thing."

"And he wasn't killed. Why do you keep saying that? He was hanged. There's a difference."

"It wasn't just a hangin'. More like he was lynched, even if there wasn't no mob involved in the proceedings."

Fargo remembered Wiley's message. It was why he'd come back to Devil's Creek. Wiley was right. When your friend got killed, you did something about it if you were able.

"The thing is," Wiley said, "there's a lot of hangin' goin' on here. A lot more than there should be."

He looked around. The tent was filled with rough-looking men eating and talking. A woman carried a bowl full of steaming potatoes, and steak sizzled on a plate in her other hand. Nobody seemed interested in Fargo and Wiley, but Wiley still looked nervous.

"You never know who might be listenin'," he said. "Do you know anything about the way law works in a minin' town?"

"I've had some experience," Fargo said.

"Well, then, you know that mostly there ain't any law *to* work. Wasn't any here when Billy came to town. That was all right for a while. People got along just fine. But after a little time went, more and more people came in, and things started to get out of hand. There were people gettin' shot and stabbed in the saloons and in the alleys, claims gettin' jumped. You know the kind of thing. So some of the citizens got together and hired a marshal. Man name of Lattner. Jack Lattner. Ever hear of him?"

Fargo thought it over and said he didn't think so.

"He's from somewhere down in the southwest. Married to a half-breed woman named Maria, part Mexican and part Apache. Or leastways he claims he's married to her. Might not be for all I know, but that ain't any of my business. Came up here to find gold, like ever'body else, I guess, but as far as I know he never found any. Tell you the truth, I think he was responsible for some of the

24

shootin's that were goin' on. He's right handy with a gun. Prob'ly shot as many men as he's hung."

Fargo said he wasn't sure what all that had to do with Billy Banks.

"This is what it's got to do with it. Billy Banks never done a thing to be hung for. Neither did most of the fellas that Lattner's strung up. The thing is that Lattner's a one-man vigilance committee. He's got the idea that he has the power of life and death over ever'body in this town, and by God, he does. He thinks he's a prophet of God."

"I guess having the power of a badge can turn a man's head sometimes," Fargo said.

"You ain't gettin' what I'm sayin' to you," Wiley told him. "What I mean is that Lattner is crazy as hell. He really does think he's one of God's prophets, sent here to cleanse the place of all the scum. That's what he says, anyway. He claims he has these visions of heaven and hell with death ridin' a pale horse and carryin' the red sword of destruction. If he sees you in one of those visions, then you might as well get ready to cash in your chips, 'cause you're gonna be dancin' on air before the week's out. It's all God's will, and God's will must be done."

"You sound a little like a prophet yourself," Fargo said.

"If I do, it's just because I've been listening to Lattner for too damn long."

"And the people in town let this go on?" Fargo said.

"Who the hell you think's gonna stand up to a crazy man who'd just as soon shoot you or hang you as say 'heighdy-do'?"

"By the way you're looking at me, I'd say you think I'm the one."

"That's right. That's why I got word to you about Billy. I knew you'd come do something about it. You're about the only hope this town's got."

"Then it's in sad shape," Fargo said.

Wiley nodded. "Amen, brother," he said.

They had finished their meal and Wiley was sopping the greasy gravy out of his plate with a piece of dry bread when all conversation in the tent came to a stop. Fargo looked over at the entrance. At first he didn't see anyone, but then he lowered his gaze and noticed that there was a man standing there.

25

A very little man.

Wiley said, "Poke Davis," and stuffed the gravy-soaked bread into his mouth.

Davis swaggered into the tent, or maybe that was just his natural gait. He was a dwarf, with broad, powerful shoulders and hands the size of mining pans. His pants were far too long for him, but they'd been rolled up to form hard, round cuffs. A tin star was pinned to his flannel shirt, the sleeves of which were rolled like the pants legs to form thick cuffs over his bulging biceps. He wore a pistol in a cross-draw holster at his waist. The gun looked like a cannon hanging there. He had a reddish beard around the fringes of his face, and his uncovered head was as bald and slick, shiny and smooth as a river rock.

He stood for a few seconds, looking around the tent. When his eyes came to rest on Fargo, they stopped. They were hard eyes, black as anthracite, and cold as the eyes of a dead lizard. Davis stared at Fargo for a while, then moved on to a vacant table. There was a wooden box sitting in one of the chairs at the table, and Davis hopped up and sat on the box.

Conversation started up again, but to Fargo it had a false and jittery sound.

"Lattner's deputy," Wiley said in a subdued voice. "I didn't tell you about him. Only man Lattner likes or trusts. Might have something to do with one of his visions for all I know."

Fargo was about to stand up to leave when somebody on the other side of the tent made a remark that cut through the buzz of talk and left the tent silent again.

"The little sawed-off bastard's so short, he'd have to jump just to kiss my ass."

"Shit," Wiley said. "That ain't good."

Fargo watched as Davis leaped down off his box. He stood with his hands on his hips and looked around. The tent was silent, the atmosphere charged.

"Who said that?" Davis asked.

There was no answer, but it was plain that Davis hadn't expected one. He walked over to the nearest table and looked at the men sitting there, all of whom were looking somewhere else—at their plates, at the sides of the tent, anywhere but at the man standing there.

Davis jabbed the closest man in the thigh with a finger thick as a sausage. He said, "Are you the one who said I was too short to kiss your ass?"

The man's face was gray as the tent canvas, and his hand shook so that the fork he was holding rattled against the thick plate in front of him.

"No, sir," he said. "It wasn't me."

"If it wasn't you," Davis said, "then who the hell was it?"

"I don't know, Mr. Davis," the man said. "I surely don't."

"You're a lying son of a bitch," Davis told him.

Moving fast as a striking rattler, he grabbed the man's forearm and started to squeeze. The fork clattered into the plate. Davis smiled up at the man, but he didn't say anything. He just kept squeezing.

The blood drained completely from the man's face. Already gray, it now turned ghostly white. The veins stood out in his neck, and he opened his mouth in a silent scream. The other men didn't try to help him. They still refused even to look in his direction.

Fargo thought the man might pass out from the pain, and he felt a little sorry for him, but this wasn't his fight. He wasn't even sure what was going on.

Then someone said, "Let go of him, you Lilliputian son of a bitch."

"Ah," Davis said with a smile, "a reference to Mr. Swift. It's good to know that an educated man lives in Devil's Creek, if not for very long."

Across the tent from where Davis stood, a man rose from his chair.

"I told you to let go of him," he said.

"Now that I know my adversary, I will, Compton. I thought it might be you. None of these other gutless wonders has the courage to stand up for a friend. Not that it was very smart of you to do it."

Davis released the man's arm. The man took a deep, shuddering breath, and for a second Fargo thought he'd fall face forward on the table. He might have, but one of his companions put out a hand to steady him.

"This ain't gonna be pretty," Wiley whispered.

Davis glanced their way, and Fargo stared straight at

him. Davis looked back toward the man he'd called Compton, who was as tall as Fargo and as thin as a poplar tree.

"You should know better than to insult me, Compton," Davis said. "You know it's not wise."

"To hell with that," Compton said. "I've had about all I can stomach of you and that goddamned Lattner lording it over this town. It's time for it to stop."

"And I suppose you're the one to stop it."

"That's right," Compton said, "and I'm going to start with you."

His hand reached for his gun. There was rustling and scraping as all over the tent people dropped from their chairs to the floor. Wiley and Fargo didn't move.

Compton was fast, Fargo thought, but not fast enough. Davis whipped out the big Colt and fired twice. Compton didn't even pull the trigger.

Davis was fast, but not accurate. His first bullet ripped through the side of the tent, but the second one did the job. It hit Compton just below the buckle of his gunbelt.

Compton sagged to his knees and dropped his pistol. Blood welled out of the wound and stained the tops of his trousers.

Two men went to help him, now that it was too late. Fargo knew they wouldn't be able to do much for him. A stomach wound didn't kill you instantly, but you were dead anyway.

"Take him to the jail," Davis said. "We'll hang him tomorrow if he lives."

For just a moment Fargo thought that someone might say or do something, but no one did. The two men who'd gone to Compton took him under the arms and dragged him out of the tent.

Davis let his gaze rove over the faces of the men. He said, "It's a damn shame to lose a man like Compton. He was probably the only man in town who'd read *Gulliver's Travels*. I would've liked to discuss the book with him. But it's too late for that now. You all saw that he drew on me. Nothing I could do but defend myself. I want every one of you to be at the hanging tomorrow to see what happens when somebody goes against the law. Is that clear?"

There was some murmuring that Davis seemed to take for assent. He nodded and got back up on his box.

"Annie!" he called out. "Bring me a steak."

"Things are worse than you let on," Fargo told Wiley over the hum of voices that began to fill the tent.

"I reckon they are. I was gonna tell you about Davis, sooner or later. He's as crazy as Lattner in his own way. I guess that's why they get along. Lattner treats him almost like a pet, and he can do pretty much what he wants to."

"I figured out that much for myself," Fargo said. "I'm pretty good that way."

"You ever read that book?" Wiley asked. "That *Gulliver's Travels*?"

"Don't believe I have," Fargo said.

"I have," Wiley said. "But I don't think I'll mention it to Davis."

"I can't say that I blame you," Fargo told him. "He might want you to discuss it with him."

"Yeah, and touchy as he is, I wouldn't want to have to do that."

"Can't say that I blame you," Fargo said.

5

As they walked the dusty street, Fargo said, "I think I need to go talk to Samuel."

"What for?" Wiley asked. "Not that I'll hold it against you for wantin' to see that woman again. She's mighty pretty. But what good's a preacher gonna do you?"

"I want to ask him about religion," Fargo said.

Wiley gave him a puzzled look. "You gone and got yourself saved, Fargo?"

"I'm not the one I want to talk about. It's Lattner."

"He's not religious. He's just crazy. I told you that."

"If a man sees visions, there must be a reason for it," Fargo said. "I want to know what it is."

"Won't help you any. Look there." Wiley pointed down at their feet. "You see that?"

Fargo had probably seen it before Wiley had. He said, "It's blood."

"Compton's blood," Wiley said. "There's prob'ly a trail of it right to the damn jailhouse. Could be your blood or my blood. Wouldn't make any difference to Lattner, nor to Davis, neither. Did you see the way he looked at you?"

"I wondered about that," Fargo said.

"It's because he don't know who you are. They watch ever'body new who comes into town. They don't want anybody messin' up what they got here."

"You say Lattner hanged Billy. Did Davis have anything to do with it?"

"He's always around, wherever Lattner is. But mostly it was Lattner's doin' that time."

"Why? What did Billy do that bothered him? You still haven't told me that."

"Not a damn thing. That's the trouble of it. If he'd killed somebody, or jumped a claim, or even tried to take Lattner's woman, there mighta been some sense to it. But that's not the way it works. If Lattner wants you dead, he just hangs you. It's something to do with his visions, like I mentioned. Billy might have had a little tussle with Poke Davis, but it didn't amount to anything. Generally, if Davis wants you dead, he just shoots you and that's all there is to it. You saw what happened with Compton."

"I can see where a man like Davis might be a little mad at the world," Fargo said. "He's probably had a rough time of it. If you're different, people don't always treat you right."

"That ain't no excuse for what he's done around here," Wiley said. "Much less for what Lattner's done."

They walked along the rough boardwalk while people all around went about their business just like always, buying supplies in the dry goods store, hauling freight, or just whittling on a stick. If Fargo hadn't known better he'd have thought Devil's Creek was a perfectly normal little town. But judging from what Wiley had told him and by what he'd seen in Annie's Place, it was a long way from that.

They came to the jail, and Fargo stopped.

"You don't want to go in there," Wiley said. "There's no call to start anything yet. You go in there, and Davis'll get you, or Lattner. Next fella to be hanged in Devil's Creek might be you. Come on."

Fargo stood where he was.

"They're just going to let that Compton fella die," he said. "And if he doesn't die, they'll hang him."

"That's right. That's the way it is around here. That's what happened to Billy. But there's nothin' you can do about it right yet. You got to have yourself a plan."

"What about a doctor?"

"What in the hell do you need a doctor for? You feelin' sick?"

"Not for me," Fargo said. "For Compton."

"We got a doctor here," Wiley said. "He's drunk most of the time, though. Prob'ly not a real doctor, either. I wouldn't trust him with a mule."

"But he's the best you have?"

Wiley nodded.

"You go find him, then," Fargo said, "and get him to come have a look at Compton."

"Won't do any good. Compton's set to hang tomorrow anyhow."

"He might be able to give Compton something to ease him a little. It's not right for a man to suffer like that."

"All right, then." Wiley turned away, then turned back and said, "You're just afraid I'll beat your time with that gal, ain't you? This is just to get me out of the way so you'll have her all to yourself."

"That's right," Fargo said. "I wouldn't stand a chance if you were around."

"That's what I figgered," Wiley said.

It didn't rain much in Devil's Creek, but at one time the road had been soft mud and the ruts had dried hard and deep with earth churned up on either side.

It wasn't far to the church, and as he approached it, Fargo could hear singing. It sounded like two people, a man and a woman, and their voices were clear and strong.

He went up to the door and looked inside. The floor was dirt, and there were rough-hewn log benches for the congregation. The benches stood on either side of a narrow aisle leading up to the altar. Samuel and Ruth stood side by side near the low altar, their faces lifted up as they sang about Jesus being the name that calms our fears.

Fargo removed his hat and stepped through the doorway. It was cool in the church, out of the sun, and Fargo could smell the dampness of the dirt floor. Light came in through a couple of windows and fell across the unpolished benches.

The brother and sister finished the verse they were singing and stopped to look at Fargo.

"Don't quit on my account," he said. "It sounded mighty good."

"We used to sing together all the time when we were young," Samuel said. "It's been so long, I'd almost forgotten the harmony."

"We'll have to sing together often now that I'm here," Ruth said. She looked pleased to see Fargo again. "What brings you back, Mr. Fargo? I'm sure you didn't come just to hear our singing."

"No, but it was worth the trip to hear it. You never told me you were a singer."

"I never really got the chance," she said, and then blushed, most likely thinking about what she and Fargo had done to take up their spare time.

Samuel was looking at her, and his face changed slightly. But if he had suspicions, he didn't mention them. He said, "If you didn't come for the singing, what can we do for you?"

"I wanted to talk to you about Jack Lattner," Fargo told him.

"Who's he?" Ruth asked.

"The marshal," Samuel said. "What about him, Fargo?"

"I've heard he's a religious man. I thought maybe you could tell me about him."

"He doesn't come to this church," Samuel said, not meeting Fargo's gaze. "And this is the only one in town. I don't know him at all."

"You know about him, though."

"I know what I've heard."

"You must've heard a lot."

Samuel turned to look out one of the windows. After a few seconds he turned back and said, "I haven't heard much. People don't like to talk about him."

It was becoming clear to Fargo that the preacher didn't want to talk about Lattner, either, and Fargo wondered why. He said, "You afraid of him?"

"Fargo!" Ruth said. "You shouldn't talk to Samuel like that. He's not afraid of anybody."

Samuel's shoulders slumped. "I wouldn't be so sure about that," he said.

Ruth put a hand on his arm. "I don't understand."

Samuel walked to the front bench and sat down. He rested his elbows on his knees and leaned forward as if he might be praying. Ruth sat beside him and put her arm around his shoulders. Fargo stood and waited.

After a while Samuel looked up. He turned to Fargo and said, "Have a seat, Mr. Fargo. I'll tell you what I can. And we may as well begin with the admission that you're halfway right. I am afraid of Jack Lattner, but maybe not for the reason you think."

Fargo sat on the bench behind Samuel. Ruth kept her arm protectively around her brother's shoulders.

Fargo said, "You're not afraid he'll hang you?"

"Hanging doesn't scare me," Samuel said. "I'm a Christian man, Fargo, and I know there's a better home waiting for me after I die. God takes care of his own. So to answer your question, no. I'm not afraid Lattner will hang me."

"Then what?" Fargo asked.

"Some people think he's crazy."

"And that's what scares you?"

"No," Samuel said. "That's not it at all."

"Then what is it?"

"I'm afraid he might *not* be crazy," Samuel said. "I'm afraid he might be in touch with something that's spiritually beyond my reach. That he might be what he claims to be, the avenging arm of the Lord."

Wiley hadn't mentioned anything about the avenging arm of the Lord, Fargo thought, unless you counted that part about Lattner's death visions and riding a pale horse.

"I don't understand, Samuel," Ruth said. "Are you telling us that there's a man here in Devil's Creek who claims to be sent from God?"

"That's right. He says he's been sent here to cleanse the earth of wrongdoers, and that the Lord sends him visions to let him know who's to die and who's to live. He . . . It's hard to explain, but he has a kind of power about him. People believe him, and nobody will stand up to him. Those who do, die. One way or another."

"I saw his deputy shoot a man today," Fargo said. "For no reason at all."

"Poke Davis. He's another part of the story. You don't know what Davis was like before Lattner came, but he wasn't anything like the man you saw today. He was a swamper in the saloons, cleaned privies, did the lowest kind of jobs. He was a sot, and more often than not he was so drunk by dark every night that he slept in the alleys with stray dogs. He was filthy and covered with sores. People treated him like a some kind of animal. They kicked him around and degraded him. I tried to help him, but there was nothing I could do. He wouldn't even speak to me. But not long after Lattner got here, he had a vision about Davis. He says the Lord came to him and told him that Davis was one of God's children, too, just like the rest of us."

"You told Davis that, too, I'm sure," Ruth said.

"I did, but it didn't seem to matter when I said it. And Lattner added a little something. He said that anybody who mistreated Davis was going to be sorry. Lattner and his wife took Davis in and cleaned him up. His sores healed. He stopped drinking and started to do errands for Lattner. The next thing we knew, he was a deputy, and with Lattner to back him up, he started to get back at the town for what had happened to him. He made people sorry for what they'd done, right enough."

"You'd think people wouldn't allow that to keep happening," Fargo said.

"If you thought that, you'd be wrong. People look at Davis's redemption as some kind of miracle performed by Lattner. And it might be, for all that I know."

"Miracles don't change the fact that he's using his badge to hurt people."

"The town asked Lattner to come here," Samuel said. "I'm sure you know that people don't like to admit they're wrong. And they're afraid of what might happen to them if they do anything to stop what's happening."

"You mean Lattner might hang them or Davis might shoot them," Fargo said.

"It's not as simple as that. There are more miracles involved. People who said things against Lattner have died from unexplained causes. Perfectly healthy people. One day they're fine, and the next day they're dead."

"That kind of thing happens," Fargo said.

"Not often, and not the way it happens here. It just happens to people who have criticized Lattner or Davis in public."

"So people think God's striking them down?" Fargo said.

Samuel sat up straighter, and Ruth's arm slid off his shoulders.

"That's right," he said. "That's exactly right."

Fargo thought he was going to have a little talk with Wiley, who hadn't even begun to explain how complicated things were in Devil's Creek.

"What about Lattner's wife?" Fargo asked.

"Maria," Samuel said. "A holy name, but not a holy woman. She has the power to lead men astray. She's part Indian, you know."

"So I'd heard," Fargo said. "Does that matter to anyone around here?"

"It matters to her. She enjoys being the wife of a marshal. It gives her a kind of power that she wouldn't otherwise have." Samuel seemed uncomfortable talking about her, and he changed the subject. "And now I have a question for you, Fargo."

Fargo nodded. "Fair enough."

"What's your interest in these people and this town?"

Fargo hadn't told anyone what he was doing in Devil's Creek, not even Ruth, but he didn't see the need to keep it a secret any longer, at least not from Samuel and Ruth.

"Lattner hanged a friend of mine." As he spoke, Fargo realized that Wiley still hadn't actually told him what Billy had done. "I aim to find out why, and if there was anything wrong with it, I'm going to try to set it right."

Samuel sat quietly for a while, gazing back out the window. When he spoke, his voice was low and powerful.

"Vengeance belongs to the Lord," he said. "Book of Romans, chapter twelve, verse nineteen."

"So I've heard," Fargo said. "But it says in the Book of Fargo that sometimes the Lord needs a little help. If this is one of those times, I'm going to see that He gets it."

"I'm afraid I don't see the humor in that, Mr. Fargo," Samuel said.

"I didn't expect you to," Fargo said.

He smiled at Ruth, who said, "You come back to visit, Mr. Fargo. On Sunday, we'll be singing together before the sermon."

"I'd like to hear that," Fargo said, without committing himself to return. "Did you find yourself a place to stay?"

Ruth looked at Samuel. He said, "She'll be staying with the Cottons for a while. They're good, churchgoing people, and they'll take good care of her. She could stay with me if I had a place, but I don't have much more than this church right now. I just camp out back, and that wouldn't be very comfortable for a woman."

Fargo thought that Samuel didn't really know much about his sister, but he didn't say so. He put his hat back on his head, settled it, and left the church.

6

Before Fargo got to Wiley's tent, he could smell pine smoke. The sun was about to hide itself behind the Bitterroot Mountains, and Wiley had started a small fire. He was warming himself by it when the Trailsman arrived.

"Be gettin' colder soon as that sun goes down," Wiley said. "Might seem like spring, but there's still plenty of chill in the night air."

Fargo dropped down by the fire and said, "Did you find that doctor?"

"Drunk as a lord," Wiley said. "I couldn't even get him sobered up enough to walk to the jail, much less do anything for Compton. Don't matter though. I heard the news in town that Compton's already dead."

"Anybody planning to do anything about it?"

"Nope. They know better. They're scared things might happen to them if—"

Wiley stopped abruptly and looked at Fargo.

"There's a few things I haven't told you yet. Things besides the hangin's."

"I know," Fargo said. "I heard about some of them from the preacher. People dying for no reason."

"Yeah," Wiley said, looking into the fire. "I didn't want to scare you away."

"You know me better than that."

"I guess I do. But I thought you might not believe me. I'm not even sure I believe it myself."

"There's something else you never got around to telling me," Fargo said. "You never told me about Billy."

"Sure I did. I told you when we were eatin'."

37

"No, you didn't. You just said that Billy turned up in one of Lattner's visions. I think there's more to it than that."

It was getting dusky dark, and the fire that Wiley had made had burned low. He looked around for a stick, and when he found one he poked at the coals. They sparked and flamed up, and Wiley laid some larger pieces of pine on the fire.

"There might be a little more to the story," he said when he had the fire burning to his satisfaction. "I guess you might as well know about it."

"It's about time," Fargo said.

But before Wiley could begin, sparks and partially burned wood jumped from the fire, and then Fargo heard the rifle crack.

Wiley heard it too, and both of them flipped onto their sides and rolled for the nearest cover. Fargo cussed when he rolled over a pinecone. He wound up behind the tree the cone had fallen from just as a bullet smacked into the trunk. He didn't see where Wiley had gone.

Whoever was doing the shooting was hidden a good way off. There was no point trying for him with a pistol, and Fargo's rifle wasn't where he could put his hand on it. There was nothing to do but wait until the shooter decided to try something else or got tired of wasting his ammunition and went away.

It took a while. Bullets buried themselves in the pine, and occasionally chunks of wood were chopped away. When the shooting finally stopped, the trunk looked as if someone had been at it with a dull ax. Fargo smelled pine gum and raw wood.

"You still here?" he called out to Wiley.

"I'm here," Wiley said from behind a nearby larch tree that was shaggy with moss. "You think your friend's gone home now?"

"Couldn't be anybody I know," Fargo said. "I just got here."

"Yeah, and I've been here for more'n a year without anybody shootin' at me. No reason for 'em to start now. Besides, there ain't no bullet holes in my tree. You must've riled somebody up pretty good."

Fargo couldn't think of anyone he might have riled. The only people he'd talked to besides Wiley were Ruth and Samuel, and there was no reason for them to shoot at him.

Wiley started to move out from behind the larch tree.

"I'd just stay put for a few more minutes," Fargo said. "By then it'll be too dark for anybody to see us if we stay away from the fire."

Wiley settled back down. He said, "You reckon that shooter could've been Davis? He gave you some hard looks while we were eatin'."

"I didn't give him any reason to shoot me," Fargo said. "I didn't say a word."

"Well, somebody around here sure don't like you. I can tell you that much."

"We'll see," Fargo said. "And speaking of eating, you got anything to rustle up for us tonight?"

"Got some bacon and beans."

"That'll do," Fargo said.

"We gonna go out and look for the shooter first?"

"It'll be too dark," Fargo said. "And he'll be long gone before we could get to where he was shooting from."

"Where was that, do you think?"

"That stand of trees off to the west. He probably had to climb one to get an angle on us. I'll have a look tomorrow."

"Think you'll find anything?"

"We'll see," Fargo said.

While they were eating the bacon that Wiley had fried up, Fargo asked again about Billy Banks. This time Wiley told him.

"It was that woman," he said. "Lattner's wife."

The bacon was hot and crisp, and the fat was sweet. Fargo chewed a bite and then said, "What about her?"

"You haven't see her yet," Wiley said. "If you'd seen her, you wouldn't have to ask."

"Since I haven't seen her, you're going to have to explain that."

"She's a mighty good-lookin' woman," Wiley said. "That black-haired gal who came here with you, she's a beauty for sure. But Maria Lattner is different. It's not just that she's pretty, which she is, in a funny kinda way. It's more than that. There's something else about her. When she looks at a man, even a dried-up old fart like me, she makes him feel like a bull moose. You know what I mean?"

Fargo had known women like that. Any one of them

could take one glance at a man and all he could think of was how she'd look with all her clothes off. And a man could tell she knew what he was thinking and that she liked knowing it.

Sometimes the thinking was as far as it went. The women liked the feeling they got from their effect on men, and they didn't need anything else. And sometimes they did. Fargo asked Wiley which kind of woman Maria Lattner was, although he'd had a hint from Samuel about her character.

Wiley drank the last of his coffee from a battered tin cup, then tossed the dregs on the ground.

"She's the second kind," he said. "The kind that needs something else. I think she needs a lot of it, and I don't think she's gettin' enough of it from Lattner. Maybe one man could never give her enough. Anyhow, I think she got some of it from Billy. He was just a kid and didn't know any better. He didn't even think about how dangerous it was. Hell, I can't really say that I blame him. I'd have done it myself if I'd gotten half a chance. You haven't seen her. When you do, you'll know."

Fargo said he already had a pretty good idea. "So you think Billy slept with her?"

"I pretty much know he did. Oh, he never come right out and said it, but he slept with her, all right. Hell, I could practically smell her on him."

Fargo put down his empty plate. There were a couple of pinecones nearby, and he tossed them into the campfire. They caught fire quickly and popped as they burned.

"So Billy slept with Lattner's wife," Fargo said, "and Lattner found out about it."

"Lattner or Davis or both of 'em. That was all it took. The next thing I knew, they had Billy in the jail, and the day after that, they hung him."

"Does Lattner like for people to be there for the hangings?" Fargo asked, remembering Davis's command to the men after he'd shot Compton.

"Him and Davis both like it. Gives 'em a good laugh, you might say, to see ever'body watchin' their friends dangle from the end of a rope. Not that there's not some in town who like it, too."

Fargo wasn't surprised to hear it. Whatever one man

could do to another, no matter how bad, there'd always be somebody who liked to watch it happen. He could feel the cold coming down from the mountains and a heavy dampness in the air.

"You can't be the only one in Devil's Creek who doesn't like what's going on," Fargo said.

"Nope. There's been some talk of formin' a vigilance committee to do something about Lattner, but nothing's ever come of it. Seems like the people who bring up the idea start dyin' off suddenlike, and the others get spooked."

"How do they die?" Fargo asked.

"Like I said, they just die. Not a mark on 'em, but they're folks who ain't been sick a day in their lives. And they ain't criminals. The only thing they've ever done wrong is talk against the marshal."

Fargo didn't quite know what to make of it all. Something was wrong in Devil's Creek, but it wasn't like anything he'd ever encountered in his wanderings. Far back in the trees, a cougar roared.

"I guess you're thinkin' you're sorry you came," Wiley said.

Fargo thought about the last week and the times he'd had with Ruth.

"No," he said, "I can't say that I'm sorry."

"Not even when you've already got somebody shootin' at you?"

"He might've been shooting at you," Fargo said. "Maybe he just wasn't a very good shot."

"It wasn't me," Wiley said. "If Lattner wanted me dead, he would've hung me by now. I shouldn't never have sent you word about Billy, Fargo. I got a feelin' that Lattner's gonna hang you before this is over with."

"Don't count on it, Wiley," Fargo said.

The morning after the shooting occurred, Fargo walked over to the stand of trees from which the shots had been fired. It wasn't hard to find where the rifleman had been. Fargo could smell crushed pine needles and see the flattened grass where the man had walked. He was a big man, and he'd scraped the bark of the cottonwood he'd climbed to get a good shot at Wiley's camp.

Fargo spotted a tuft of animal hair caught on a rough

41

place on the tree trunk. He reached up, pulled the hair loose, and rubbed it between his fingers. A porcupine sat about ten yards away and watched, not in the least afraid of Fargo.

"Did you get a good look at him?" Fargo asked, but the porcupine didn't have any answers. He watched Fargo for another few seconds and walked away in the awkward-looking way that porcupines have. Fargo watched him go, but he didn't really see him. He was wondering about the hair that he still held.

Buffaloes didn't climb trees, Fargo thought, and anyway, he hadn't seen any buffalo around. Even if there were, the hair had been too high for the animal to have rubbed against the trunk and left it there. But somebody wearing a buffalo robe might have climbed up there, though it would have been awkward. The lowest limb of the tree was just within Fargo's reach, so the climber had been tall. Fargo remembered his feeling of danger coming from behind him, but he didn't think it could be Tom and his friends. They were safely dead and buried at the trading post. So the buffalo hair was one more mysterious thing for him to think about.

Fargo walked out of the trees. To the west, the Bitterroot Mountains were gray in the morning light, and white clouds were scattered along their tops. The place where Fargo stood was at a slightly higher elevation than the town, and he looked at the helter-skelter set tents and buildings. Smoke rose above some of them, and people were beginning to stir. Fargo was sure that on the creek men were already panning, hoping to find the nuggets that would be the beginning of their fortune.

He went back to Wiley's camp. The older man was scrambling eggs in the big iron skillet in which he'd cooked last night's bacon.

"These things cost as much as that steak we had yesterday," Wiley said. "If a man really wanted to make himself some money here, he'd get him some chickens. How many of these eggs you want?"

"Two should do me. I'll pay you for them."

"Now, don't start that stuff with me, Fargo. I'm the one asked you to come here, and I'll feed you any time I can. I wasn't complainin' about that. I was complainin' about the people who might as well stick a pistol in your ribs when they sell you an egg. Come on over here and eat."

He scraped the eggs into two plates, and he and Fargo sat near the fire to eat them.

"You decided yet what you're gonna do about Lattner?" Wiley asked.

Fargo said that he still wasn't sure he was going to do anything. "Lattner's the law, and from what you've told me, some of the people here support him, no matter what he's done. I'm not going to fight a whole town just because Billy Banks went and got himself strung up."

"He didn't get himself strung up. He just dipped his wick in the wrong place. If they hung ever'body that did that, you would've been strung up in half the towns in the territories, and don't tell me you wouldn't."

Fargo grinned and ate his eggs.

When they'd finished breakfast and cleaned up the plates, Fargo told Wiley that he was going into town.

"I think it's time I met the marshal," he said.

"You want me to go with you?"

"I appreciate the offer, but there's no use in Lattner knowing that we're friendly."

"Davis has already seen us eatin' together. And he's the kind who never forgets anything. He already knows."

"Maybe. But he didn't have any reason to tell Lattner. If I don't run into him at the jail, he still won't."

Wiley looked dubious, but he said, "Well, if that's the way you want it, go ahead. But you stay out of trouble, you hear?"

"I'll try."

Wiley sighed and shrugged his shoulders.

"I've heard that one before," he said.

Fargo did try, but he was the kind of man who just had a natural disposition for trouble. If he didn't go looking for it, it came and found him. This time it came in the shapely package of Maria Lattner.

Fargo saw a woman going into the jail, but he was too far away to tell much about her. When he got to the jail, she was still inside, and he thought he might as well go on in. There didn't seem to be any reason not to.

But Lattner wasn't there. The woman was the only person inside when Fargo went through the door, and the second he saw her, he knew that she was Maria Lattner, and he knew that Wiley had been right about her. She wore a loose dress that somehow did nothing to hide the fact that she had an ample figure: large breasts, wide hips. She had a heart-shaped face, dusky skin, and thick black hair that hung down her back in a long braid.

There was certainly nothing remarkable about her appearance. There were probably several women in Devil's Creek who were prettier, including Ruth, but the force of Maria Lattner's sexuality hit Fargo like a fist. There was something primitive about it, and it seemed to come off her in waves. He imagined her writhing beneath him, clawing at his bare back with her fingernails as she urged him on to greater and greater exertions. Fargo felt short of breath, as if his chest had been constricted.

Poor Billy, Fargo thought. He never stood a chance.

"Are you looking for someone?" Maria asked.

Her voice was low and husky, and she sounded amused. Fargo didn't doubt that she knew exactly what he was thinking.

"I'm looking for the marshal," he said, trying to keep his voice level.

"So am I. He's my husband, but it doesn't look like he's here. Is there anything I can do for you?"

There was just the slightest emphasis on the word *anything*. Someone listening to the conversation might not have noticed, but Fargo did. The word seemed loaded with invitation.

"I don't think so," he said, but they both knew he was lying.

"He could be at home," Maria said. "That's where I'm going. You can come along with me if you want to."

There was nothing that Fargo wanted to do more, because he knew from the tone of her voice that Lattner wasn't at home and wouldn't be for quite a while.

"I'd better not," he said. "Your husband might not like it."

"I haven't seen you around town before," she said. "What's your name?"

"Skye Fargo. Most people just call me Fargo."

"That's what I'll call you, then. Are you sure you don't want to walk me home, Fargo?"

Wanting didn't have a thing to do with it. Fargo said, "I'd better not. I think I'll just wait here for a while."

"If that's the way you want it, then."

She brushed past him as she left the jail, and though she didn't actually touch him, Fargo would have sworn that sparks jumped between them.

When she was gone, Fargo sighed deeply. There hadn't been a woman who'd made him feel that way in a long time. Ruth had been passionate and wild, but compared to Maria Lattner, she was practically a virgin.

Fargo went outside and took a deep breath of the fresh air. He could see Maria moving away up the street, but he forced himself not to look after her. He was afraid he might try to follow her home. He didn't think he'd stick around the jail, either. He didn't want to meet Lattner, not just then. Even though it was still early in the day, what he needed was a drink.

As he walked toward the Trail's End, he saw a wagon at the end of the street. It was being pulled by two horses, and as it passed an alleyway, a large gray cat ran out into the street, pursued by six or seven dogs, all of them barking and straining to be the first to catch the cat.

The cat was intent only on getting to the other side of the street and didn't care what was in the way. It ran directly under the two horses pulling the wagon, and the dogs followed close behind. The horses were spooked. They reared up, throwing the driver from his seat, and when their hooves hit the ground, they started to run. The wagon wasn't loaded, and it was surprising how fast the horses could pull it.

Fargo and everyone else nearby stepped to the edge of the boardwalk for a better look. The wagon bounced wildly from side to side, and the driver was up and running after it. There wasn't a chance in hell of catching it, and before he'd gone far, he stumbled and fell. He sat in the dust, yelling curses after the runaway wagon.

When it was almost to the place where Fargo stood, he felt something nudge his back. Before he could turn to see what it was, he got a firm push and found himself falling from the boardwalk.

He wasn't quite as startled as whoever had pushed him probably hoped, but he was off balance and stumbling forward when he hit the street.

He heard the pounding of hoofs, the rattling of the wagon, the snorting of the horses. He knew without having to look that he was right in the path of the runaway.

He managed to right himself and make a half turn, and then the horses were on him.

7

Fargo didn't have time to think, only to react. He was right between the horses, and when the first one's head went by him, he grabbed the harness and let himself be jerked off his feet and pulled along with the team. He could smell the sharp tang of the animals' fear-sweat mixed with the dust from the street as his boot heels bounced over the rough ground. He tightened his grip on the harness with his left hand and reached for the horse's mane with his right. When he had a good hold, he started to pull himself up on its back. It was quite a strain at first because he could use only his arms, but then he hooked his heel over the animal's back and was able to pull himself up easily.

It was almost as bad as riding an unbroken bronco, though the horse wasn't trying to throw him. It was just scared. Fargo couldn't get hold of the reins, so he lay down along the horse's neck and tried to keep from falling off while he whispered soothing words into its ear.

The horse wasn't soothed, and neither was its harness pal. They continued to run, and Fargo wondered how far they could go before they gave out. He wondered if he could hang on that long.

He didn't have to find out. One of the back wagon wheels hit a rut hard and came loose. It went rolling off to the side, and the back of the wagon on that side dropped down and threw things out of kilter. There was more drag on the horses, and they slowed down noticeably. Fargo kept whispering to the one he was on, and this time it seemed to have some effect. Or maybe both horses were just tired. They ran for another fifty yards, slowing down so much that Fargo could have gotten off if he'd wanted to. But he didn't want to spook them again. He stayed for the whole ride, twenty or thirty yards more. The horses came to a gradual halt, then stood snorting, their sides heaving.

Fargo slipped to the ground. They were nearly to Samuel's church, but there was no sign of either the preacher or Ruth.

Looking back toward town, Fargo could see that a number of people were headed in his direction. He supposed they wanted to see if he was still in one piece.

The first man to reach Fargo said, "That was a hell of a ride you had. I thought you were gonna get yourself killed. You shouldn't have tried to stop 'em."

"I didn't try anything," Fargo said. "Somebody pushed me into the street. I was just trying to keep from getting run over."

"Who the hell would do a thing like that?"

"That's what I'd like to know," Fargo said.

Walking back to Main Street, Fargo didn't pass anyone he recognized, not that he'd expected to. Most people hadn't bothered to come out to the wagon to check on him. Now that the excitement was over and it was pretty clear that nobody had been hurt, they'd lost all interest.

Fargo got back to town, past the jail, and on toward the saloon. He needed that drink now more than he had before his ride. But he was always alert to what was going on around him, and something on the other side of the street caught his eye. It was a figure in a beaver hat.

Fargo crossed the street in front of a wagon loaded with logs and pulled by a couple of wall-eyed mules. They were moving at a leisurely pace and paid him no attention at all, but they did slow him down a little, and by the time he got to the other side of the street, there was no sign of anyone wearing a beaver hat.

Fargo looked around and saw an alley between two buildings nearby. He walked quickly to the alley and looked down it to see if there was anyone there. He thought he caught a glimpse of someone turning the corner at the end and going behind the buildings.

Fargo debated about whether or not to follow. He hadn't actually seen anybody, and maybe the shooting of the previous evening had started his imagination to working too hard. Or maybe his encounter with Maria Lattner had done that. Not to mention his brush with the team of horses.

But things like that had never distracted Fargo in the past. He'd always been able to depend on his senses, and they'd told him he'd seen somebody. And he certainly hadn't imagined the hat. He decided to investigate.

He walked down the alley and paused at the end. Before he turned the corner, he pulled his Colt from the holster. Then he took a quick look around the corner to see if anyone was waiting for him.

No one was. Fargo walked along behind the buildings, looking down to see if there were any prints, but the ground was too hard to take impressions. He smelled garbage and the odor that came from a couple of privies. But he didn't see anyone.

That didn't mean much. There were other alleys, and the man in the beaver hat could be back on the street by now. Or he could have gone into one of the buildings through the back door.

Fargo thought again of Tom. The buffalo hair in the tree and the beaver hat both fit, but Tom was dead, and Fargo didn't believe in ghosts. Even if there was such a thing as a ghost, it wouldn't be solid enough to push a man of Fargo's size into the street.

Sliding his pistol back into the holster, Fargo turned up an alley and went back to the busy street. It was past time for that drink.

There were several people in the Trail's End, but it wasn't crowded at that time of morning. The place smelled of liquor and sweat and the sawdust covering some of the floor to soak up spilled beer and liquor. On one side of the big main room, a man slept with his head on the table, his hand wrapped around the empty bottle beside his head. One of the whores Fargo had seen when he rode into town, the blonde with the scar, sat at a table talking to a man dressed like a bottom-dealing gambler. Four men played cards at another table. Fargo recognized two of them from the game Wiley had been in, and Fargo wouldn't be surprised if Wiley showed up later to join them again.

What did surprise Fargo was the sight of Poke Davis standing up at the bar. He wasn't tall enough to see over the top of it, so he was standing on an overturned box. He had a glass of whiskey in his hand, and when Fargo came through the batwing doors, Davis turned to see who had entered.

Fargo walked over to the bar and asked for a beer. He didn't stand near Davis, and he didn't look in his direction. When the bartender brought the beer, Fargo paid him and sipped it slowly, looking at the whiskey bottles lined up in front of the cracked mirror behind the bar.

It wasn't long before Fargo heard a thud of boots on the floor as the dwarf hopped off his box. There was a scraping noise as Davis dragged the box along the floor until it was beside Fargo. Davis got the box squared away to his satisfaction and jumped up on it. He set his whiskey glass down on the bar with a click, but Fargo still didn't look at him. Davis didn't seem to mind. He met Fargo's eyes in the mirror.

"You're new in town, ain't you?" Davis said.

"That's right," Fargo said.

"I saw you yesterday. You were there when Compton tried to shoot me."

"Is that the way it was?"

"You should know. You were there, all right. You and Wiley Rawlings. You saw the whole thing."

Fargo didn't have any comment on that.

"People are always saying things like that about me," Davis said. "About how short I am, I mean."

"Are you short?" Fargo said. "I didn't notice."

"That's pretty funny," Davis said, but he wasn't laughing. He wasn't even smiling. His dead eyes stared at Fargo's image in the mirror. "Maybe people say things about me being short because they think they have some kind of an advantage on me. They generally find out different."

"Like Compton did," Fargo said.

"Yeah, like that," Davis said. He smiled thinly and took a sip of whiskey. "Is that the way you are?"

"I don't take your meaning," Fargo said.

"Do you think you have some kind of advantage on me?"

"Like Compton, you mean?"

"Yeah, like him."

Fargo wasn't ready to confront Davis yet. He said, "I

don't think anything. I just came in here for a beer. Not for a conversation."

"You too good to talk with a short man?"

"I'm not too good to talk with anybody. I just don't feel like talking right now."

Davis put back his head and drained his glass. He slapped the empty glass down on the bar and eyed Fargo again.

"What's your name?"

Fargo told him.

"Mine's Poke Davis. I'm the deputy marshal here. Anybody gives me any trouble, I give it right back."

"Like with Compton," Fargo said.

"I don't like you, Fargo," Davis said. "You got a smart mouth on you, you know that? What happened yesterday was Compton's fault. He said something about me that I couldn't let pass."

"How do you know it was him? He's not the first person you accused."

"That's what I mean about your smart mouth," Davis said. "You could find yourself in big trouble if you stay in town. This isn't the kind of place you should stay around very long. I'd leave in a hurry if I were you."

Fargo finished his beer. He was tired of talking, and he was tired of Davis.

"You're not me, though," he said.

He turned to leave the saloon, but he hadn't taken more than a step when a man wearing a marshal's badge shoved through the batwing door.

He was tall and wide, so big that he almost blotted out all the light from the street. He had a round head and a big white hat. His chest strained the buttons on his shirt, and his belly strained them even more. His eyes, unlike Davis's, were not dead at all. They were bright, mad eyes, and they burned in his seamed face as if there was a fire lit behind them. The most striking thing about him was the scar around his neck, the scar left behind long after the burn of the hang rope disappeared. No one had mentioned that mark to Fargo. He'd have to have a word with Wiley about that.

"Morning, Marshal," Davis said at Fargo's back.

Lattner didn't reply. He let his wild eyes roam around the room until they came back to settle on Fargo.

"I know you," he said.

His voice was hoarse, as raspy as if he were gargling a grassburr.

"I don't think so," Fargo said. "I haven't been in town long enough to meet you."

"Won't be here much longer, either, if you have any sense," Davis said. "I told him he'd be better off to get on out of town, Marshal."

The marshal ignored Davis. He continued to stare at Fargo, his eyes boring into Fargo's as if trying to see inside the Trailsman's head. By that time, everyone in the room was looking in their direction. Fargo noticed that the blond whore had moved away from the man she'd been talking to.

"Your name is Skye Fargo," Lattner said, "and you are an abomination unto the Lord."

"Goddammit, you're right, Marshal," Davis said. "I thought the same thing myself. An abomination is just exactly what he is. I guess we'll have to hang the son of a bitch, then." He hopped down off the box, pulled his pistol, and thumbed back the hammer. The sound echoed off the mirror behind the bar. "Time for you to get your ass to the jail, Fargo. Either that or I can shoot you right here."

"Not yet," Lattner said. "The time for his punishment is not yet come."

"Hell, why not?" Davis asked. "We have him right here. No use in letting him go. I can take him right on down to the jail and save us a world of time and trouble."

"I've had no vision about him yet," Lattner said. "I never hang a man unless the Lord sends me word."

"Damn," Davis said. He lowered the hammer of his pistol and shoved the weapon back into its holster. "I don't see why we can't get it over with before he runs off and hides."

"I won't be hiding," Fargo said.

"Then you'd better be gone," Davis said. "The marshal won't mess around with you once he has a vision."

Lattner stepped aside and said, "You can go now, Fargo. Your freedom at this moment is a gift from the Lord. Pray that we never meet again."

"I'm not much of a one for praying," Fargo said.

"That's only one of your many sins," Lattner told him. "And soon the Lord will lay His hand on you and have you count your transgressions one by one as you stand before His mighty judgment seat."

"It might not be as soon as you think," Fargo said.

"If you don't watch your mouth, it'll be sooner," Davis said at his back.

"Don't be too sure of that," Fargo said, and he walked past Lattner and went outside.

8

Fargo blinked in the bright sunlight. Off in the distance, over the roofs of the buildings, the Bitterroot Mountains rose gray and high, the snow on top sparkling in the brightness. Below the tree line the ponderosa pines, larches, and firs were darkly green. Up and down the street, people went about their daily business as if nothing about their little town was different from any other, as if their marshal didn't talk like a crazy revival preacher and the deputy didn't want to hang just about anybody he met.

The batwing doors opened and swung shut behind Fargo, and there was the sound of a light step on the boardwalk.

"Scary, isn't he," said a voice at Fargo's shoulder.

The Trailsman turned his head slightly and saw that the blond whore was standing just behind him and to his right.

"He talks a lot like a preacher I heard once," the woman continued without waiting for Fargo to comment, "but he's not like any other preacher I ever knew."

Fargo didn't ask how many preachers she had known or in what connection.

The woman moved so that she could see Fargo and he could see her as well. A breeze swept along the street and blew her hair into her face. She pushed it aside and said, "My name's Venus, by the way."

Fargo knew that most women in Venus's line of work preferred not to use their real names. He said, "I'm glad to meet you, Venus."

"My, aren't you the proper gentleman? You didn't seem so glad to meet the marshal. You had any dealings with him before?"

"No," Fargo said. "I never had the pleasure."

Venus laughed. "Well, now you have. And he called your name, even if he hadn't met you. You want to buy me a drink?"

Fargo looked back at the saloon. "In there?"

"Oh, no. That wouldn't be a good idea, not with the marshal and his little pardner still inside. But that's not the only place in town to get a drink, you know."

Fargo had noticed a couple of other places, none nearly as grand as the Trail's End. He said, "Where did you have in mind?"

"You come on along, and I'll show you."

Venus started to move away, but before she could take a step, Fargo put out his arm for her to take. Venus blushed, the scar on her face standing out lividly against the whiteness of her skin, but she laid her hand lightly on his arm.

"You don't think you're being a little overly polite?" she said. "Folks here know what I am. They won't think highly of you for being so friendly to me."

She was right. Some people stopped their conversations to look at Fargo as he and Venus proceeded down the boardwalk.

"Doesn't matter to me what they think or don't think," Fargo said. "Now, where are we going?"

Venus smiled faintly. "Just up the street. To Honoria's tent."

"I don't know Honoria," Fargo said.

"I work for her," Venus told him. "There's more at her place than just beds. A man can get a drink there if he wants one. He can get other things, too, but you probably know that." She gave Fargo a sidelong glance. "Not that a man like you would ever have to go to a place like Honoria's."

Fargo smiled to let her know that he appreciated the compliment. He said, "Do you think it's a good idea for Lattner to see you with me? If he has a vision of me, he might see you in it, too."

Venus shook her head and said that she didn't think so. "He never seems to see women. Just men. Which is kind of funny when you think about it. If he's as much against sinning as he says he is, you'd think the first place he'd get rid of would be Honoria's."

Fargo had a feeling that Lattner wasn't against sin so much as he was against particular sinners. But it was too soon to know yet just what was going on in Devil's Creek. Sometimes things had a way of changing while you looked at them, like an image in water when the wind blew across it.

They reached Honoria's tent, and Fargo stood aside to let Venus go inside ahead of him. A little sunlight filtered in through the sides and top of the tent, but there was no other illumination. It was a very big tent, and there was a smell of dust, warm canvas, and musty bedclothes. There were a couple of tables with chairs around them in the front. The rest of the tent was partitioned off on each side by blankets hanging from a rope, and a corridor ran down the middle of the tent, with more blankets partitioning off sections that Fargo figured contained beds or cots where private business could be transacted. There didn't seem to be much going on at the present, it not being the time of day for that sort of business, and Fargo didn't see any of the other women.

"Everybody's asleep in the back," Venus said in answer to his unspoken question. "Or else they're at one of the saloons, like I was, looking for men who might like to come by a little later for a toss. Miss Honoria will sell us a drink."

She raised her voice and called out for Miss Honoria, and a woman answered, asking what the hell Venus wanted. Venus told her, and she and Fargo sat at one of the tables. After a couple of seconds an amply built woman came from the back of the tent with a bottle of whiskey and three glasses. She set the bottle and glasses on the table and looked Fargo over.

"Goddamn, Venus," she said. Her voice was as deep as a man's. She wore a cotton gown and robe, and her dark hair was streaked with gray. Her arms were large and round, and she had bright black eyes. "You got yourself a mighty fine-lookin' one this time. He might be too much of a man for a youngster like you. I might have to take him on myself."

"His name's Fargo, and he's not here for that," Venus said. "He's going to buy me a drink, and we're going to talk."

"Good thing I brought an extra glass, then," Honoria

56

said. "He'll have to buy me a drink, too. I like to have payin' customers here, not talkers."

She sat down at the table with them and poured whiskey into the three glasses. Honoria knocked hers back in one swallow and wiped her mouth with the back of her hand.

"Usually I like for my customers to pay in advance, Fargo, but I needed that. You can pay now."

Fargo put the money on the table, and Honoria gave him an approving smile before sweeping the coins into her hand. They clinked together and then disappeared somewhere inside her robe.

"You seem like a nice fella, Fargo," she said, "prompt with your payment and all, so I'll let you and Venus have a private talk. If you want anything else, you give me a call, you hear?"

"I hear," Fargo said.

Honoria gave him an exaggerated wink, heaved herself out of the chair, and left him and Venus sitting at the table.

"I guess you know why I brought you here," Venus said when Honoria was gone.

"No, I can't say that I do," Fargo told her. "I figured you'd let me know soon enough."

Venus took a sip of the whiskey and set her glass down on the table. She looked into the glass rather than up at Fargo.

"I knew somebody," she said after a few seconds. "Somebody you knew, too. His name was Billy Banks."

"What makes you think I knew anybody by that name?"

"Because he talked about you," Venus said. She reached up and ran her index finger along the scar on her face. "He said you were one of the best trailsmen he'd ever known and that it was a privilege to travel with you."

Fargo didn't disbelieve her, but he wasn't sure why Billy would have been saying something like that to a whore. Venus looked up from the glass and into Fargo's eyes. He saw for the first time that her eyes were a clear cornflower blue.

"I know what you're thinking," she said. "You're polite to me, but you're wondering why your friend Billy would be talking to a whore."

She ran her finger along the scar again, and Fargo saw that it was a fairly recent mark.

"Poke Davis did this," she said. "He would've cut my throat if it hadn't been for Billy."

Fargo took a drink of whiskey and said, "Billy stopped him?"

"That's right. I was in the saloon one day, just like today, and Davis came over to me. He thinks that because he's the marshal's deputy that he can have any woman he wants. And generally that's true. But that day I was sitting with Billy. Billy was like you, nice and polite, and he didn't treat me like a whore. He just talked to me about things, things he liked or had done or wanted to do. That's why I was with him. For just a few minutes I could forget that any man can have me if he's got the money."

That sounded like Billy, all right, Fargo thought. He said, "Davis didn't like that?"

"Davis didn't care one way or the other about Billy. He was just interested in me. But I wasn't interested in him, not right then. Because I was sitting in a chair, the top of his head was just about on a level with mine. He grabbed me by the hair, jerked me back, and had a knife in his hand quicker than you can blink your eye. Billy was just as quick, though. He knocked Davis's hand away, and instead of cutting my throat, he cut my face."

Venus put her finger to the scar yet again and traced it from just beneath her chin up her cheek to where it disappeared into her hair.

"So Davis didn't kill me, and to tell the truth the scar he gave me hasn't even hurt my business that much. Lots of men like somebody who looks a little different. They'd never tell their friends that, but they do."

"What did Davis do next?" Fargo asked, hoping to get her back to her story. He didn't really care about learning what men wanted from her.

"He went for me again, but Billy was out of his chair by then, and he grabbed Davis by the wrist and threw him all the way across the saloon. He hit his head on the bar and bounced off. He didn't get up for a while after that, and by the time he did, Billy and I were gone."

Fargo figured that was the "little tussle" Wiley had mentioned. It wasn't so little, after all, but it might explain why Davis hadn't just shot Billy down on the spot. He hadn't been capable of it.

"I guess there's a reason you're telling me this," Fargo said.

"There's a reason, all right. You were Billy's friend, and I'd hate to see you end up the same way he did. The way you were talking to Davis in the saloon, I'd say you were mighty close to it."

"You heard Lattner," Fargo said. "He's the one who has the visions."

"That's right. But who do you think puts them in his head?"

Now the talk was getting interesting, Fargo thought. He said, "You believe somebody's controlling Lattner?"

Venus finished the whiskey that was in her glass and looked wistfully at the bottle.

"Honoria doesn't mark the bottle like some people do," she said, "but she knows how much is in there right down to the very last drop."

Fargo said he'd pay for another drink, but Venus told him that she wouldn't have one. She said, "I don't really know what there is about Lattner that makes him different. There's some who think he's just crazy, and there's some who believe he's having heaven-sent visions just like he says he is. But it seems to me that somebody's putting ideas in his head, and if that's the truth, I'd bet my money on Poke Davis. People in this town pushed him around worse than if he was a whore before Lattner came here, and maybe now he's getting back at everybody by using Lattner some way or the other. Anyway, that's all I wanted to say to you, that you'd better be careful, or you'll be doing a rope dance just like Billy did."

"Do you know a man named Wiley Rawlings?" Fargo asked.

"He's a card player. I've seen him in the saloon. He was a friend of Billy's."

"Have you ever talked to him about Billy and what happened to him?"

"No. I don't know him to talk to, and he's never paid me a visit here. Billy might've told him, though. I wouldn't have any way of knowing about that."

Venus stood up. So did Fargo.

"I thank you for the drink," she said. "And for treating me like a decent person. I know what I am, but now and then I like to feel different."

"Did you ever think you might just be a decent person?" Fargo asked.

"No," she said. "Not in a long time."

Fargo left Venus at the tent and started walking back toward the jail, where he'd left his horse earlier that morning, but he couldn't quit thinking about the fact that Lattner had known his name. As best Fargo could figure it, there was only one way the marshal could have found out, which would mean that Maria Lattner had lied about her husband's being away from home. She'd said she was going there, and when she did, she must have told Lattner about seeing Fargo at the jail.

And it seemed to Fargo that if anybody was influencing Lattner, as Venus thought, then that someone was a lot more likely to be the marshal's wife than his deputy. Maybe the fact that Fargo had refused her implied invitation to visit her had upset her, and so she had told her husband that Fargo was a sinner and an abomination.

Fargo decided that he'd find out. And he had another reason to talk to her as well. He wanted to ask her about Billy Banks.

Across the street at a dry goods store, a man was loading some supplies into the back of a wagon. Fargo walked over to give him a hand. When they'd finished, the man thanked Fargo for his help, and added, "If you ever need the return of a favor, Bob Hensley's your man."

Hensley had a seamed face with watery eyes and a three-day beard, and he appeared sensible enough. So Fargo said, "I could use a favor right now."

Hensley turned his head aside and spit a stream of tobacco juice on the street.

"I wondered why a man'd walk across the street to help out somebody he didn't know," Hensley said, wiping his mouth on his sleeve. "I was hoping you did it out of the kindness of your heart, but I should've known better. Well, what the hell. I said I'd return the favor, and I will. What do you want me to do? Kill somebody for you? Burn down his house?"

Fargo laughed. "It's not quite that big a favor," he said. "I was just going to ask you where the marshal lives."

"Now, why would you want to know a thing like that?" Hensley asked, giving Fargo a suspicious look.

"I'm new in town," Fargo said. "I thought I'd drop by and pay my respects to the local law."

"You must be really new here if you thought a thing like that. Marshal Lattner ain't exactly sociable."

"I wanted to ask him about a friend of mine that was here for a while," Fargo said. "Fella named Billy Banks."

Hensley spit again, then looked at Fargo through narrowed eyes.

"You know what happened to your friend?" he asked.

"I've heard some stories. I don't know if they're true."

"Most anything you hear about this town is true," Hensley said, "whether you think you can believe it or not. Your friend found that out the hard way. I don't think my neck would fit a rope, and I'd just as soon not have what happened to him happen to me. Or to you, either, since you were kind enough to help me out, even if you did want something for it."

"I still don't have what I wanted," Fargo reminded him.

Hensley looked down the street to where the gallows stood beside the jailhouse. Then he returned his gaze to Fargo.

"I hate to be the one to tell you what you want to know," he said. "I'd feel bad if you was to wind up hanging in the breeze down there because you went by the marshal's house."

"You don't have to worry about that," Fargo said.

"That just shows how much you know about this town," Hensley told him. "Anyway, the marshal's prob'ly down there at the jailhouse right now. Why don't you go by there and see?"

"I'd rather try the house," Fargo said.

"Yeah, I thought you might. Well, at least I tried to help you out."

"And I appreciate it," Fargo said. "Now, where does the marshal live?"

Hensley told him, and added, "You might even be really unlucky, friend. The marshal's wife might be home."

"You mean lucky, don't you?" Fargo said. "I've heard she's a fine-looking woman."

"Yep," Hensley said. "I've heard the same thing. Seen

9

The marshal's house was easy to find since there weren't many houses in Devil's Creek. Most people were miners, and the ones who owned a business usually slept in the back of their stores. But a few people had built places to live that were more or less intended to be permanent, and Marshal Lattner was one of them. The houses were at the south end of town, behind a couple of blocks of commercial buildings and tents. They were in a neat row, and according to Bob Hensley, Lattner's was the second one from the end. Like most of the other buildings Fargo had seen, it was built of raw lumber that still smelled green. There was a little whitewashed fence around the yard, which was mostly hard-packed dirt that looked as if it had been swept clean.

Fargo went in through the gate and walked up on the porch. He was about to knock on the door when it opened. Maria Lattner stood in the doorway, looking at him.

"Well, Mr. Fargo," she said. "I didn't think I'd be seeing you this morning. But I'm glad you changed your mind and stopped by for a little visit. Do you want to come in?"

Fargo had allowed himself to forget the hint of sexual excitement in the woman's every look and word, but the memory of it returned with a rush when he saw her. He thought that Hensley might very well have been right about this visit being unlucky. But Fargo went inside anyway, finding himself in a small parlor with curtains on the window, a couple of plush-bottomed chairs, and a small table with a lamp sitting on a lace doily. There was a faint scent of perfume in the air.

Maria closed the front door behind him and said, "My

husband's not here, if it's him you're looking for. He won't be back for the rest of the day."

Fargo didn't even have to wonder why she'd added that last bit of information.

"I've already seen him," Fargo said. "To tell you the truth, I'm here because I saw him."

"And knowing he wouldn't be here, you came?"

Fargo ignored the innuendo and said, "Not exactly. I came because of something he said to me."

"You mean he sent you?" Maria said, not appearing to believe it.

"No," Fargo said. "He doesn't know I've come."

As soon as the words were out of his mouth, Fargo regretted having said them, but it was too late to take them back.

Maria smiled. "I'm glad to hear that."

The words were harmless enough in themselves, like most things that Maria said, but they carried implications that Fargo understood far better than he wanted to.

"Why don't we sit down?" Maria said. "We'd be more comfortable, don't you think?"

Fargo wasn't sure he'd ever be comfortable in her presence. He doubted that any man would, not for very long. But he sat in one of the chairs. Maria sat in the other and said, "Now, tell me what you really came for."

Her sexuality was so overpowering that Fargo was tempted to tell her that he'd come to drag her into the bedroom, but he restrained himself. He said, "I came because when I met your husband, he already knew my name."

Maria laughed. "That's not surprising to me. Jack seems to know things like that more often than not. He's an unusual man."

"So I've heard. But I thought there might be a simple answer to the question of how he knew who I was."

"You did?" Maria raised her eyebrows. "What answer would that be?"

As she spoke, Maria turned slightly in the chair, stretching just the slightest bit. But it was enough to make her clothing emphasize the curve of her heavy breasts. Fargo's throat suddenly felt tight and a little dry.

"He found out my name from you," he said. "I told you it this morning at the jail."

Maria smiled and stretched, more obviously and more languorously this time. Fargo felt his groin stirring in response. His mouth got drier. If Billy had gotten into trouble because of this woman, it was entirely understandable.

"He's not here, so I couldn't tell him. And he won't be here, either. Didn't I mention that?"

"You mentioned it. But maybe he was here earlier."

"No, and I haven't seen him to tell him anything. You could ask him about that, but he won't be here for a good while."

Again, the words were innocent enough, but the implications weren't. Fargo said, "If he wasn't here, how could you have told him my name?"

"That should be pretty obvious. I didn't tell him. He doesn't need me for things like that. It's like I said: He just knows."

It was beginning to seem as if just about everybody in Devil's Creek believed that Jack Lattner was more than just an ordinary man. Fargo, however, wasn't convinced. He'd known fakers before. No need to mention that, though. He said, "Is that all he knows?"

"What do you mean?"

"I mean, does he know when you have visitors?"

"Are you afraid he'll find out you were here?"

"No," Fargo said. "I'm not. But I heard that a friend of mine visited you, and things didn't turn out so well for him."

"What's your friend's name?"

"Billy," Fargo said. "Billy Banks."

The smile slipped off Maria's face, and she didn't say anything for a while.

"I remember Billy," she said at last. "He was a friend of mine, too."

"He must not have been a friend of your husband's," Fargo said, "seeing as how he got himself strung up."

"That didn't have a thing to do with me," Maria said. "Billy got into a fight with Poke Davis. Do you know who that is?"

"I've met him," Fargo said.

"He's Jack's deputy. Billy got into a fight with him and nearly killed him. That's what caused all the trouble. That's why Billy got himself hanged."

Fargo hadn't heard the story exactly that way, but he didn't see any need to say so. Maria wasn't going to change her version of it based on anything Fargo told her. And for all he knew Venus had been the one who exaggerated, not Maria.

"Isn't this beautiful weather?" Maria said, abruptly changing the subject. She stood up and walked to the window. "It's very warm for this time of year, don't you think?"

Fargo said he guessed it was.

"Yes," Maria said. "And I've found that I'm much more comfortable when I don't have on quite so many clothes, if you know what I mean."

Fargo felt his own temperature rise a couple of degrees. He was pretty sure he knew exactly what she meant.

"I think you and I could get to be good friends," she said. "Very good friends. Most people are afraid to come here because of my husband, so I hardly ever have anyone to talk to."

Fargo got the clear impression that she didn't really mean *talk*. He said, "I can see how that might happen, what with people getting hanged around here so often."

"Not all that often, but then Devil's Creek is a lawless town. Now and then someone is going to be found doing the wrong thing." She smoothed her dress down over her breasts. "But never hanged for doing the right thing."

She turned from the window and walked past Fargo. He could feel the heat coming off her as if he'd been sitting by a fire.

"I'm going into the bedroom," she said. "I'm going to get comfortable. Would you like to get comfortable, too?"

Fargo didn't say a word. He sat in his chair like a statue and watched her go. When Maria got to the door, she looked back and said, "I'll be very comfortable in just a minute. Why don't you wait and come in when I call you?"

Fargo nodded, and Maria went into the room and closed the door.

This is a big mistake, Fargo thought. *It could be the very thing that got Billy's neck stretched, and even if it's not, it's still not smart. I should get up right now and walk out of here.*

But he knew he wouldn't. He sat right where he was,

and after a while he heard Maria call him from behind the closed door. Thinking about her had caused his rod to stiffen, and he got up with some difficulty. Then he walked to the door and opened it.

The bedroom was small, though it was big enough for the bed that Maria was lying on. She had drawn the curtains, but there was still plenty of light for Fargo to see her. And she was quite a sight. Her skin was dusky, and her breasts were even larger than he had expected, with dark areolas and nipples that stood up hard and erect. As he stood there taking her in, she let her right hand stray over her nipples, down her stomach, and into the dark thatch of pubic hair. She looked into his eyes as she slid her fingers into the wiry tuft and allowed her middle finger to caress the slit at the junction of her legs. Then the finger disappeared, and her eyes closed in pleasure.

When she opened them again, she said, "I thought you were going to get comfortable, too, Fargo. What are you waiting for?"

It was a question Fargo couldn't answer, and he hastily shed his clothes, leaving them in a pile on the floor as he joined Maria on the bed.

As soon as he lay down beside her, she rolled to him and embraced him. Her skin was hot, and she pulled him against her so that his rigid pole was pressed tight between them.

"Feels like you've got something nice down there," she said, her mouth close to his. "I'll have a look in a minute."

Then she kissed him. Her mouth was like a furnace, and her hot tongue darted between his lips and found his own. Her pillowy breasts pressed into him, their blazing tips branding his chest. When they broke apart, she rolled to the side. She reached for his shaft and began to run her hand up and down its length, letting her fingernails tease it from top to bottom.

Fargo got busy with his own hand, sliding it between her legs and letting it glide along her inner thighs.

When he touched her sweet spot, Maria shuddered. She released his pole and lay back, saying, "Yes, yes. Don't stop. Please."

Fargo continued to move his finger gently over the distended knob while lowering his head to kiss Maria's breasts. He ran his tongue slowly over the fiery nipples, then took one of them into his mouth, sucking it in and tickling it with his tongue. Each time he sucked, Maria quivered. After a minute or so, she reached down and took his wrist to help him rub her at just the right tempo. Her hips rotated slowly and sensuously, and soon she was pushing and pulling on his wrist, causing his finger to move faster and faster.

"Ahhh," she said. "Ahhhhh."

Her hips rose from the bed, higher and higher, until she was bouncing up and down. She released Fargo's wrist because he didn't have to move his hand any longer. She was doing all the work herself, reaching such an intensity of excitement that she flung her head from side to side, her hair whipping across her face.

Her breath came short and fast, and Fargo thought she was going to explode under his hand, but at that moment she brought herself under control, stopping just short of completion. She moved Fargo's hand and said, "It wouldn't be right for me to finish so long before you're ready. Let me do something for you."

Fargo couldn't deny her, and she rolled over and took his pulsating rod between her lips. Then she inhaled it, or seemed to. Fargo had never felt anything quite like it as his entire penis disappeared into the overheated cavern of Maria's mouth and slipped farther back than he would have thought possible. The action and the surprise sent a stinging thrill through Fargo from his scrotum to his feet, practically causing his toes to curl backward. Then Maria did something with her throat that caused it to constrict, and Fargo's back arched. She did it again, and Fargo could barely control himself. One more time, and he'd lose control.

Maria seemed to sense that the moment had come, and she slowly let him slide out of her mouth. When he was completely free, he lay on his back, breathing heavily. Maria said, "You liked that. I could tell."

Fargo didn't answer. He wasn't sure he had the strength. Maria didn't mind. She threw her leg over him and straddled him, leaning over to let her breasts dangle just above his face. She jiggled them, and Fargo turned slightly so that he could tongue her left nipple.

"Oh, yes," she said. "That's good."

She reached between her legs and took hold of his stiff manhood. Holding it by the root, she slid the tip of it up and down, allowing it to brush lightly over her taut pleasure button.

"Oh, God," she said. "Oh, God, that's good. That's good."

She stopped and held him steady for a second, then thrust herself back and down on him hard, burying his entire length in her slick, hot body. She ground herself against him, pressing her body down hard. Her bottom lip caught between her teeth, she twisted and moaned above him.

Setting his hands on her hips, Fargo turned her over until he was positioned between her legs. He slid slowly out of her, right to the tip of his throbbing shaft, then pushed it back inside her equally slowly. After several of the easy thrusts, Maria said, "Now, Fargo. Give it to me now!"

She rocked under him and worked her inner muscles to pull him deeper and deeper while squeezing him at the same time. She clawed at his back.

"Faster, Fargo! Faster! Fill me up! Now! Now!"

Fargo could hold back no longer. Pleasure took hold of him as white-hot waves of ecstasy crashed over him while she trembled beneath, her own climax racking her entire body with spasms.

When they were finally done, Fargo slipped out of her and lay back on the bed beside her.

"You're so much of a man," she said. "I didn't know I could feel like that."

"You made me feel pretty good, yourself," Fargo said, thinking that she knew more tricks than most any woman he'd known.

She turned on her side and ran a hand over his body, seeming to notice for the first time the scars that he carried.

"You've been shot," she said. "More than once."

"And missed a lot more times than I've been hit," Fargo said.

"You must lead a dangerous life."

"Depends on how you look at things. There are lots of things more dangerous than a bullet."

"I'm sure there are, like whatever made this scar right here." Her finger traced a path along the cicatrix. "Whatever it was, it must have been big."

"It was a bear," Fargo said, "and it was big all right." He remembered the bear and the way its claws had torn him. "But there are things even more dangerous than that."

"What things would those be?"

"I got a feeling you're one of them," Fargo said. "I've traveled a lot of this big country, and the truth is that there's nothing more dangerous than a beautiful woman."

"I don't think you'll find me dangerous, Fargo. Not after the way you've treated me."

"I hope not," Fargo said, but he was thinking about Billy Banks and the way he'd died.

"You don't have to worry," she said, reaching for his penis and taking it in her hand. "Will you look at that? I didn't think I'd see that thing rise up again for a month, the way I treated it. But it's standing up like a soldier at attention. Maybe we can put it to use again. Why don't we give it a try?"

"Why not?" Fargo said, and so they did.

10

Wiley was standing outside his place with his hands on his hips when Fargo rode up. The tent was, as Wiley put it later, "torn all to hell." Wiley's supplies were scattered around haphazardly, cornmeal and sugar poured on the ground, bacon dumped in the dirt. His bedding had been set afire and burned. The tent had been ripped with a knife.

"Son of a bitch!" Wiley said as he looked at the devastation.

Fargo slipped off the big Ovaro and said, "Somebody doesn't like you a hell of a lot."

"I slipped off to catch some chow and that goddamned marshal must've paid me a visit while I was out," Wiley said. "Him or his sawed-off deputy. Or both of 'em."

"You'd better watch how you talk about the deputy," Fargo said. "I don't think he takes to people who call him short."

"I didn't say the little bastard was short. I said he was sawed-off."

"Yeah, I can see how he'd like *sawed-off* better." Fargo picked up a stick and poked at the cornmeal. "I don't think you'll be using this to make bread with again."

Wiley kicked his charred bedding. "Those bastards. Sorry low-down bastards."

"You don't know they did it," Fargo said. "Let me have a look around."

While Wiley stood aside and cussed, Fargo went over the ground. What had happened was easy enough to read. There had been only one rider, and he'd ridden his horse right up to the tent before dismounting and going inside.

71

He'd thrown everything out and then shredded the tent with his knife. The burning of the bedding had probably come last.

"Don't see why the sons of bitches didn't just burn the tent, too," Wiley said while Fargo was investigating. "That way they coulda ruined it completely. The way it is, I might be able to sew this one up."

"There was just one man," Fargo told him. "Maybe he felt sorry for you, didn't like to think of you having to sleep out in the cold."

"Just one man? Must've been that goddamned Davis, the sneaky little son of a bitch."

"You mean sawed-off?"

"Sawed-off, little, whatever the hell he is. He's a sneak and a coward."

"I don't think it was Davis," Fargo said.

"Why not? You got some way to tell how tall the bastard was?"

"We've already gone over why Davis or Lattner wouldn't sneak around to do something to us. They'd just hang us, not tear up our tent."

"Our tent? What the hell do you mean *our tent*? That was my tent, and nobody else's."

"I didn't mean to be laying claim to your tent," Fargo said. "What I'm trying to tell you is that I think whoever did this was after me, not you. If I'd been staying somewhere else, you'd still have your tent in one piece."

"Don't see how the hell you can say they was after you, considerin' it's my tent and things that're ruined."

"If you can calm yourself down, I'll show you," Fargo said. "Come over here."

Wiley muttered a few more cuss words and kicked his burned bedding a time or two, then walked over to where Fargo stood. Fargo pointed to the tent that lay on the ground at their feet.

"You see that?" Fargo said.

"Hell, yes, I see it. It's what's left of my tent. You think I don't know my own goddamned tent?"

Wiley was like most people, Fargo thought. He looked, but he didn't really see. Fargo supposed that was all right if you played cards or panned gold for a living, but it wouldn't do if you were a trailsman.

"I'm not talking about the tent," Fargo said. "I'm talking about what's on the tent."

"There ain't nothin' on it. It's just been cut to rags, is all."

"Let's get a little closer," Fargo said, kneeling on the torn canvas.

Wiley knelt beside him, knees creaking.

"Don't you laugh, you son of a bitch," he said when Fargo glanced at him. "I might be old, but I can still whip a kid like you."

"You'd have to catch me first," Fargo said, "and with those knees you couldn't catch a one-legged horse."

"You'll get old one of these days," Wiley said. "Just you wait. Then you'll be sorry for teasin' an elderly gentleman like me."

"Maybe so, but right now, look at this."

Fargo pointed to a cluster of dark hairs caught in the ragged edge of the canvas where it had been ripped by the knife. Wiley leaned closer. He said, "Looks like it might've come from a buff. You tellin' me that a buff ran through here and did this?"

"No. I'm telling you that maybe a dead man did. He wears a buffalo robe."

"A dead man? You mean a ghost?"

Fargo shook his head. "No ghost did this. I'm beginning to think I'm not as good a shot as I used to be."

"Well, you never know a man's dead until you stick him in the ground and cover him over. You think that man did this? One you say you shot?"

"I don't *say* I shot him. I did shoot him." Fargo went on to tell Wiley about the trouble at the trading post and how it had turned out.

"Well, all I can say is that he's gettin' around mighty damn good for a dead man who's not a ghost."

"I don't know that it's him," Fargo said. "I haven't seen him in the flesh, not since I got here."

"You oughta go to the marshal, tell him what's happened. Tell him the fella's tryin' to kill you. Maybe Lattner'll have a vision about him and put him out of your misery."

Fargo didn't think it was likely, but it might be worth a try just to see what Lattner's reaction would be.

"There's something about Lattner I've been meaning to ask you," Fargo said.

"What's that?"

"Who tried to hang him?"

"You saw that scar, then," Wiley said. "Nobody knows the answer to that for sure. His story is that he was strung up for rustlin' down in Texas, but that he was innocent of the charges. The Lord sent a lightnin' bolt to strike the tree where they was hangin' him. It split the tree to kindlin', and it killed two of the posse that was hangin' him. Burnt all the hair of another one of 'em. Left Lattner with that scar, but they cut the rope off him and let him go on his way. He claims that day was the start of his knowin' who was doin' wrong and makin' him the right arm of the Lord."

"Makes a good story," Fargo said. "You believe it?"

"Hell, no. Do you?"

"You never can tell. Maybe that lightning strike fried something inside his head."

"Fried or not, he's nuttier than a squirrel, and that's for certain. But I can't be worryin' about him. I got to get this tent back together."

"You want me to help you?"

"I can handle it. You better go see the marshal and tell him about this ghost that's tryin' to kill you, not to mention messin' up my camp."

Fargo said he'd do that. He mounted the Ovaro and turned its head toward town.

Marshal Lattner didn't appear to care a thing about Wiley's tent or about the man who seemed to be stalking Fargo.

"You show him to me, and I'll deal with him," Lattner said.

It was late afternoon. A slant of sunlight came in through the front windows of his jail office, and a faint smell of fear and sweat drifted from the back of the jail where the cells were. Fargo thought he could hear something back there, whimpering maybe, but the cells were hidden by a locked wooden door with a small barred opening in the top. If the smell or the sounds bothered Lattner, he didn't show it. He was sitting at his desk, chair tilted back on two legs, hands linked atop his hard round belly, looking at Fargo and explaining why he wasn't going to do anything about the destruction of Wiley's property.

"It could be that it happened the way you say," Lattner went on, "but it could be that it was just a bear that came through and tore things up. We get a lot of bears around here—brown bears, grizzly bears, both kinds. They get into camps all the time and cause trouble. That's what people get for leaving food out where the bears can get to it."

"It wasn't a bear," Fargo said.

"Maybe it wasn't. Then again, maybe it was." Lattner let the chair come down on all four legs. There was a hollow echo from the plank floor. "You can look at it any way you want to, but the fact of the matter is that I haven't had any vision of wrongdoing against any tents. There's a lot worse evils in this town than that, and I've got my hands full with them."

Lattner's eyes shone with fanatical fervor, and Fargo got an uneasy feeling that there was something going on that he didn't know about.

"What kind of evils?" he said.

Lattner leaned forward and rested his elbows on the desk as if he were tired, or dizzy. With a nod toward the cell block, he said, "Whoring, for one thing. Women selling their bodies to men for cash money. That's one of the abominations of the earth according to the Book of Revelations. I had a vision about it just today, and I'm going to bring it to an end here in this little town. This place may be named for the devil, but I'll bring it to God before I'm done."

"What happens between a man and woman is their own business," Fargo said. "Did you ever think about that?"

"That's not from the Bible."

"It's from the Book of Fargo. You might want to think about it."

Lattner stood up, a bit unsteadily. He shook his head and glared at Fargo. The hang-rope scar stood out from his neck and seemed almost to pulse like a vein. Lattner clenched and unclenched his hands.

"You're making mock of the Good Book," he said. "I could hang you for that."

"You're not going to hang anybody," Fargo told him.

"That's where you're wrong," Lattner said. "Now you go on and get out of here before I get anymore upset with you. I don't want to hurt you before your time comes."

Just as Fargo was about to say that he didn't want to leave just yet, the door of the jail opened behind him and threw a block of light onto the floor.

"Well, look who's here," Poke Davis said. "Want me to shoot him, Marshal? I can put one in the back of his knee. Wouldn't kill him, but it'd hurt like hell and keep him out of our way for a while. Maybe for a long time if he was to be crippled permanently."

"We don't back-shoot anybody," Lattner said, "not even a heathen like this one. You can go now, Fargo, and don't bother coming back. If I want you again, I'll come looking for you."

Fargo turned and looked down at Davis, who didn't have the pistol pointed at the Trailsman's knee at all. The Colt was aimed straight up at Fargo's face. Davis was smiling, and Fargo could tell he wanted to pull the trigger.

"You heard what he told you, Fargo," Davis said. "If we want you again . . ."

". . . you'll come looking for me," Fargo finished for him. "I heard him, all right. I don't think you'd be too happy if you found me, though."

"You bet I would," Davis said. "I'd be happy as hell. I'd be happy to put a bullet right in your eye."

"It's not going to work out like that," Fargo said. "So don't get your hopes too high. And remember what that book the marshal likes so much has to say about the meek inheriting the earth."

"Gotta be somebody to run it for 'em when they do," Davis said. "And that'll be me and the marshal."

"I'm not looking forward to that," Fargo said.

"Maybe not," Davis told him. "But you might as well get used to it. Now move on along before I forget what the marshal told me about shooting you."

Fargo nodded and left, but he was worried about what Lattner had said. And he was wondering about those noises back in the cells.

Having told Wiley that he'd meet him at Annie's Place for supper, Fargo started in that direction when he left the jail. As he walked past Honoria's tent, the madam came out and accosted him. Before he even had a chance to greet her, she grabbed him by the arm, and Fargo came to a stop. Fargo could smell whiskey on her breath and sweet-scented powder on her body.

"This is your fault," Honoria said in her deep, liquor-roughened voice.

"What is?" Fargo said.

"What the marshal's done, that's what."

"It won't last long," Fargo said, remembering Lattner's comments. "Nobody's going to be able to shut down a whorehouse in a mining town. There are too many men willing to pay for what you have here, and they won't stand still if Lattner tries to cut them off from it."

"Oh, he's too smart to try something like cutting them off for what they want that much," Honoria said. "If he was just trying to shut me down, I wouldn't give it a second thought. But it's a lot worse than that."

Fargo got that uneasy feeling again. He asked how bad it was.

"Bad as it can get. The bastard's going to hang Venus."

Fargo was convinced that Lattner was crazy, but even a crazy man wouldn't hang a woman just for being a whore. Or at least Fargo didn't think so.

"Why would he do something like that?" he asked.

"He says he's going to make her an example, and an example like that's what'll put me out of business. Won't be a woman in my place that'll open her legs if she thinks she's going to get hanged for it."

It sounded to Fargo as if Honoria was a lot more worried about her business than she was about Venus. He said, "When did he arrest her?"

"Him and that little shadow of his came in about an hour ago. Took her right out of the place and hauled her off to the jail. They said she was a shameless whore and an abomination to the Lord."

Lattner seemed to get a lot of pleasure out of calling people abominations, Fargo thought.

"He said they'd hang her day after tomorrow," Honoria went on. "Right there on the gallows by the jail. I'm surprised they don't just hang her tomorrow and have it over with."

"They probably want to make sure there's a good crowd," Fargo said.

"You think there won't be a good crowd for hanging a woman? There'll be a crowd for sure. You don't see a thing like that every day. Hell, everybody in town will be there."

"Why did you say it was my fault?" Fargo asked.

"Because you walked down the street with her. Anybody with any sense knows you don't keep company with a whore where people can see you. I've been in this business for . . ." She stopped abruptly and gave Fargo a coy look. "For a long time. I know the proper way to do things, and I taught Venus better than that. But she never could resist a good-looking fella like you. I guess she wishes she'd stayed away from you, but it's too late for that."

"She just wanted to talk," Fargo said. "You know that. You know we didn't do anything else."

"I know it, you know it, and Venus knows it. Hell, maybe even the marshal knows it. But she's the one he picked out to hang, and if she'd kept herself away from you it never would've happened. You should've known better, yourself."

"There's no harm in talking, or in walking along a street. No harm in doing more than that if that's what you want to do."

"Not in a town that's run by Jack Lattner. There's plenty of harm in just about anything he says there's harm in. I might as well pack up and get out of town. There won't be any money to be made here."

"You're just going to let him hang Venus and not do a thing about it?"

"What the hell can I do?" Honoria said.

"You could talk to your customers. You could tell them what's happening. Maybe they'd be upset enough to do something about Lattner."

Honoria thought it over for a second. Then she said, "I could do that, all right. It could be that some of 'em will be pretty upset when they find out what they'll be missing. If it works, fine. If it doesn't, I'm getting out of town. I don't want to get hanged."

She turned away and went back into the tent, leaving Fargo standing there. He remembered what Venus had said earlier that day, that if Lattner was so much against sinning, the first place he'd close would be Honoria's. And Fargo had thought then that Lattner didn't mind sinning as much as he minded particular sinners. This time he'd singled out Venus, and Fargo couldn't help but think Honoria was right: she'd been singled out because of her association with Fargo. But why hang her? Why not hang Fargo? Because she was an easier target? Or was there more to it than that? As seemed to be happening a lot lately, Fargo had far more questions than answers.

He walked on down the street to Annie's. He hadn't had anything to eat since Wiley had fixed eggs that morning. Even thinking about Venus's situation couldn't keep Fargo from feeling hungry.

Wiley was standing in front of Annie's tent when Fargo got there, and they went in together. The place was full of miners, all of them chewing and talking at the same time. Fargo and Wiley found a seat, and while they were waiting for their steaks, Fargo told Wiley what had happened with Lattner and later with Honoria.

"Don't tell me you're gonna just sit back and let him hang that gal," Wiley said.

"I don't plan to. How would you break her out of that jail?"

"I wouldn't waste my time tryin'. There just ain't no way. The rest of this town might be tents and green lumber, but that place is built solid."

"I guess we'll have to try something else, then," Fargo said.

"What else is there?"

"First, we'll talk to the preacher," Fargo told him.

"What the hell good will talkin' to the preacher do?"

"You never know," Fargo said.

11

It was fully dark when Fargo and Wiley left the tent. Annie had lit several lanterns inside, and Fargo could see their mellow glow through the canvas as he walked away. The steak had been tender this time, and Wiley explained that it was elk. "Beats beef all to hell. I could hunt us one, but we'd never be able to use all that meat."

Fargo was going to visit Samuel, but Wiley declined the invitation to go with him. He said, "You go ahead if you want to, but leave me out of it. I'm not much on visitin' with preachers. I'm not much on goin' to church a-tall, not even when there's a good-looking woman there, if you want to know the truth about it. Those Bible thumpers give me the fantods."

"This one might not be so bad," Fargo said, though he wasn't entirely convinced of that. He hadn't quite figured out why Samuel didn't want his sister to stay with him. It seemed funny to Fargo for someone to look for other lodgings for his blood kin, even if the accommodations at the church weren't quite up to snuff.

"I don't care if he's good or bad," Wiley said. "I'd just rather find something else to do. I can go back to my place and clean up some more around my tent, or what's left of it. Or maybe I can think of a way to break your friend Venus out of the jailhouse, since I don't think you'll get any help from the preacher. Say what you will about 'em, good or bad, preachers ain't in the habit of savin' whores."

"I thought that was their job," Fargo said.

"You thought wrong, then. I never knew a preacher who'd pour holy water on a whore if her dress was on fire, no matter what they say about forgivin' and forgettin'."

"It's still worth a try," Fargo said.

"Then you'll have to be the one to try it."

Wiley didn't say any more, and when Fargo mounted the Ovaro, Wiley sauntered on down the street to the jail. When he reached it, he disappeared into the shadows, and Fargo figured Wiley was going to look it over to see if there were any weak spots. Fargo didn't think there was any way to get into it or to get Venus out of it, not if Lattner and Davis were guarding the place. Wiley would find out for sure, though, and maybe Samuel could think of a better way to get things done. As Fargo had told Wiley, talking to the preacher was worth a try.

Ruth was at the church with her brother, and she seemed uncommonly glad to see Fargo. He was sure she would've kissed him if her brother hadn't been around. Her demeanor changed, however, when Fargo explained why he was there.

Samuel, who hadn't appeared all that happy to see Fargo in the first place, was even less pleased after hearing Fargo out. He didn't seem at all interested in Venus and her predicament. In fact, when he spoke, his voice was cold, and he seemed to side with the marshal.

"She's a scarlet woman," he said. "You can't expect me to intervene on her behalf. I'd lose all respect in town if I did."

"I don't believe that," Fargo said. "I think people would respect the hell out of you if you stood up to Lattner."

"That's an unfortunate turn of phrase," Samuel said.

Fargo looked around the church. It looked a little different. Maybe it was the lantern light, or maybe it was because the place had been cleaned up some since his last visit. He thought Ruth might have had a hand in that. He turned to face Samuel and said, "Unfortunate or not, it's right for a man of the cloth to stand up for the downtrodden. As somebody said once, 'If you did it for one of the least of these others, you did it for me.'"

Samuel gave him a skeptical look and said, "Is that also from the Book of Fargo?"

"Book of Matthew . . . I think, but then you'd know that, being a preacher. The question is, do you just know it, or do you follow it?"

Ruth stood by quietly, watching the two men. Fargo glanced her way, but she looked off to the darkness in a corner of the church as if she didn't want to get involved in the discussion. Fargo didn't blame her if she felt it wasn't her place to tell her brother what to do.

"As I understand it," Samuel said, avoiding the question Fargo had asked, "you want me to rouse up the town in defense of a whore. You might even think your heart's in the right place, but you're wrong. Anyway, I can't see anybody in town listening to me. That woman's the worst of sinners, just the kind of person that Lattner would single out because he thinks he's the right hand of the Lord, put here to cleanse the town. I can't help you, Fargo, as much as I'd like to."

Half the preacher's face was in shadow, and it was as if half the man's feelings were hidden by the gloom. Fargo had the impression that Samuel wouldn't like to help at all, no matter what he said. It seemed more like he was downright happy to see another sinner get her just reward. Honoria hadn't been excited about helping, either, but at least she'd said she'd do something. Fargo thought it was a hell of a note when a whore was more willing to help somebody out of trouble than a preacher was.

He told Samuel and Ruth good-bye and left the church. He was about to mount his horse when Ruth came outside.

"I'm sorry about Samuel," she said. "I don't know what's gotten into him. He used to be the kind of man who liked to help people."

"You could remind him of that," Fargo said.

The moon had risen pale and white over the valley, and Ruth's face looked almost ghostly in its light.

"He's not the same," she said. "Not the way he was when he left home. He was going to come here and start his little church in a place that he said needed him. He wanted to help people. When the gold fever hit, he wrote to me and Moses. He knew that Moses had never had much luck at anything he turned his hand to, but he thought that mining might be the chance Moses had been looking for. He sounded happy and eager for us to come out here and join him. He was glad enough to see me when I got here, but he's been distant ever since."

"How do you like the Cottons?" Fargo asked.

"They're fine people, but it's not like staying with your own family. I'm worried about Samuel."

She might have said more, but before she could, Samuel came out of the church.

"It's a beautiful night," he said, "but it's not really proper for two single people to be enjoying it together, especially when the woman's husband has been dead for such a short time."

Fargo wondered what Samuel would think if he knew just what Fargo and Ruth had been enjoying every night on their way to Devil's Creek.

"I've done my grieving for Moses," Ruth said. "He was a good man, but he's gone now. I have to think about myself."

Fargo thought that she'd better not have set her cap for him. She was a fine woman, and he'd taken a lot of pleasure in their romps, but that didn't mean he was thinking about giving up the life of the trail for the life of a miner or a farmer or anything else that would require him to live in a house and do chores and be a part of a community. That kind of life was fine for some folks, but not for him. He'd wither up and die as fast as a cougar in a cage.

"You should set your mind on higher things," Samuel told his sister. "Come along. I'll see you to the Cottons' place."

He took her arm and turned her away from Fargo. They started walking, and when they were twenty or so yards away, Ruth turned back to look at Fargo. There seemed to be an appeal in her look, but he didn't know exactly what she could be appealing for. He climbed up on the Ovaro's back and rode off to see if Wiley had found out anything about the jail.

Wiley and Fargo sat by the little campfire Wiley had built. Wiley had boiled some coffee, and they were drinking it while Wiley told Fargo what had happened while he was having a look at the jail.

"You shoulda been there, Fargo," Wiley said, picking up a stick and stirring the campfire. "Those whores came marchin' down the street, ever' single one of 'em that works for Honoria. It was a sight to see, I'll tell you that."

"I imagine it was," Fargo said. "But did it do any good?"

"Hell, no. I ain't never seen Lattner so mad. His neck turned red and swole up so much, I thought he'd bust. That hangin' scar looked like a snake had coiled around him. And that Davis wasn't much better. He would've shot somebody if Miz Lattner hadn't been there to stop him."

"What was she doing there?" Fargo asked.

"I guess she brought the marshal his supper. She didn't have any sympathy for them whores, though. She told 'em all to get on their way and that they were a affront to the decent women of the town."

"Decent women?"

"Yeah, it's kinda funny, her sayin' that, considerin' that she led Billy on like she did."

Fargo could have told Wiley that Maria was a bigger hypocrite than she had appeared, but he didn't see the point in it. He said, "Did the women leave?"

"Oh, they left, all right, but not before they gave that marshal an earful. I bet he ain't been called that many names in his whole life." Wiley paused and took a drink of coffee. "He took it, though, much as it pained him. I give him credit for that. He didn't try to arrest any of 'em or hang 'em. And he didn't let Davis shoot anybody, but that might've been because of his wife."

"He didn't let Venus go, though."

"Nope. He didn't have any intention of doin' that, he said. He's gonna hang her, and that's that."

"Unless we can stop him," Fargo said.

"Yep. But there ain't much chance of us doin' that. I looked all around that jail, and it's solid as one of those mountains over there."

Wiley gestured with his tin coffee mug in the general direction of the Bitterroots that rose high and dark on the other side of the valley. The snow on their peaks looked pallid in the chalky light of the moon.

"There's always a way," Fargo said. "We just haven't found it yet."

"Ain't likely to, either. You'll just have to kill Lattner and end it that way."

"You're a hard-hearted son of a bitch when it comes to having somebody else do the shooting," Fargo said. "Why don't you just kill him yourself?"

Wiley laughed good-naturedly. "I don't blame you for

bein' a little hostile. You know I can't shoot a man in cold blood anymore than you can. I asked you to come here 'cause I thought you might figger out what's goin' on and put a stop to it, one way or the other. You don't have to shoot anybody if you can find a better way to get rid of Lattner, which you ain't done yet, by the way."

"I'm working on it," Fargo said, but he really didn't have any ideas of what to do. He'd go to town in the morning and talk to Honoria. Maybe she'd get her girls to go back for another try. Fargo might even be able to help her with that. Or maybe they'd already been more effective than Wiley thought. If they had, Fargo wanted to find out.

"I see you didn't get your tent sewed up," Fargo said.

"That's a big job," Wiley told him. "It'll take a while. Won't hurt me to sleep out under the moon tonight. You reckon our ghost'll pay us another visit?"

Fargo had seen no signs of anyone around the camp, ghost or man, but then he hadn't had any warning the other times they'd been attacked.

"No way to say if he'll show up or not. I guess we'll just have to sleep with one eye open."

"I can do that," Wiley said.

Nothing happened that night, but shortly after Fargo and Wiley had eaten breakfast, they had a visitor.

"I thought I'd come by and see how you were doing," Ruth said.

She was driving a little one-horse buggy that she'd borrowed from the Cottons. Samuel wasn't with her.

"How'd you know where to find us?" Wiley asked.

"Everybody knows about you, Mr. Rawlings," she said, giving him a big smile. "You're a famous man in these parts."

Wiley's scrawny chest swelled a little. He said, "That's the truth. Why don't you hop out of that buggy and I'll rustle you up some breakfast? I had eggs yesterday, but we ate 'em. If a man wanted to get rich here, he could just buy him some chickens. I got sow belly, though, and coffee."

"I've eaten," Ruth said, "but I thank you for the offer."

She started to get out of the buggy, and Wiley hustled over to offer her his hand and help her down.

"What happened to your camp?" she asked when she was standing beside him.

"Seems like me and Fargo got us an enemy," Wiley said. "From what Fargo tells me, you might know him."

Ruth looked at Fargo. He said, "You remember Tom."

"Him?" Ruth said. "But he's dead."

"That's what I thought," Fargo said. "But he might be harder to kill than I thought he was."

"Have you seen him?"

"Not quite. But there've been signs of him."

Ruth shook herself, and there was a frightened look in her eyes. "I didn't know I was in danger."

"I don't think you are," Fargo said. "I think I'm the one he's after. I'm the one who shot him."

"I can't believe he followed us all the way here."

It was pretty hard for Fargo to believe it, too. The more he thought about it, the harder it was. But he couldn't think of anybody else who'd be trying to kill him.

"There's something else I need to talk to you about," Ruth said. She looked at Wiley. "If you don't mind."

"Don't mind a-tall. Just make out like I'm not here and go on with whatever you've got to say. I'm used to being ignored when Fargo's around. Nobody cares about a dried-up old cuss like me with a young buck like him standin' by. I remember when I was young. There was many a young gal that tried to get me off to herself for one reason or another."

Ruth smiled and touched his arm. She said, "I'm sure that's true. You're still a handsome man. But I just want to talk to Fargo, not romance him."

"You do whatever it is you want to do," Wiley said, clearly pleased with the compliment. "I'll just do a little cleanin' up around here."

He went over to his mangled tent and held up one side of it, peering through one of the long cuts.

"Why don't we go for a walk?" Fargo told Ruth. "We can talk, and Wiley can get some work done."

She nodded, and they strolled off into the trees in the direction of the creek. Ruth didn't seem to want to talk, though she'd said that's what she'd come for. Fargo didn't encourage her, and they walked in silence in the shade of the pines and cottonwoods.

"I want to talk to you about Samuel," she said.

"Go ahead."

"I told you that he's changed, but there's more to it than that. He seems almost obsessed with sin and sinners. When he's with me, that's about all he talks about."

"He have anything specific in mind?" Fargo asked, thinking about the nightly lessons he'd given Ruth. He damn sure didn't think of it as a sin, but you could never tell about preachers.

Ruth knew what he meant. She said, "He doesn't know a thing about us."

"That kind of talk can get mighty tiresome all the same," Fargo said.

"It's not that it's tiresome. I don't mind that kind of talk, usually. He's a preacher, after all, and sin's naturally what he talks about now and then. But this is different. He's always talking about God's judgment on sinners and how God's punishment is being visited on Devil's Creek."

That sounded familiar. Fargo said, "He ever mention the marshal?"

"Some of the time. I'm never quite sure whether he thinks the marshal's doing God's work or the devil's, though."

Fargo wasn't sure about that, either, though he thought he had a pretty good idea. He said. "What about the marshal's wife?"

"Samuel seems to hate her. He never says why, and I'm almost afraid to ask him."

"He was glad to see you, but didn't seem like he wanted you to stay with him," Fargo said. "He put you off with the Cottons. Any idea why?"

"He said it was because he was just sleeping in the church, but that can't be it. He has a little lean-to in back, and it's big and comfortable enough. Samuel has all his things in there, and I stayed in worse when Moses and I were making our way out here. I could have stayed there for a while at least. He's family, after all. But he doesn't want me around. I don't know why."

"Maybe Samuel has things to do," Fargo said, knowing that was a weak excuse for sending your sister to live with somebody else, and at the same time wondering just what those things might be.

"He does," Ruth said. "He says he's praying and fasting. He doesn't do it in the church, though. He goes off in the woods. He says that while he's gone, there wouldn't be anybody at the church to protect me if anything happened."

"What could happen in a church?"

"I don't know. I asked him, and he didn't answer me. He just said it was for the best that I stay with the Cottons."

Fargo frowned. Samuel's excuses didn't add up.

"I don't want you do worry about me," Ruth said, appearing to know his thoughts. "There's nothing anybody can do about it. I just wanted to talk to somebody, and you're a good listener." She smiled. "That's not all you're good at, either. Better than Moses ever was, that's certain. Maybe I didn't really want to talk at all. I might've had other things on my mind."

"I hope so," Fargo said. "When I see you, I know I do."

"And I'm glad. But I have to tell you that I think there's another reason Samuel wanted me to stay with the Cottons."

"What's that?"

"They have a son. He's a few years older than me, but he seems to be a hardworking man. He's not a miner. His father has a store in town, and he works there. I think Samuel is trying to play matchmaker."

Fargo didn't know what to say to that.

Ruth smiled. "I don't have any illusions about you, Fargo. You're not the kind of man who's ever going to marry and settle down. You're always going to be out on the trail, heading somewhere or other and never staying anyplace very long. I'm surprised you've stayed in Devil's Creek as long as you have."

"I haven't done what I came here for," Fargo said, relieved to know that Ruth didn't have designs on him. "You could do worse than marry a storekeeper. If he does things right, he should make a pretty penny from all the miners here."

"We'll see what happens," Ruth said. "I'd feel better about everything if Samuel weren't acting so strangely."

Fargo would have felt better too, but he didn't say that to Ruth. He said, "I guess we'd better get on back. Wiley will be worried about us."

"Do you really think that?"

"No," Fargo said. "I don't."

* * *

Wiley had done some sewing on the tent, and by the time Fargo and Ruth returned, he said that he had it just about ready to set up again.

"Might have to sleep outside another night, though," he said. "I'm not as handy with a needle as I once was."

Ruth offered to help him out, but he turned her down.

"That heavy canvas is more work than I'd ask anybody to do for me. It's tedious, but I can handle it." He gave Fargo a shrewd look. "What did you two have to talk about for so long?"

"The good preacher," Fargo said. "Let's go into town and see if we can have a little talk with Honoria."

"Who's Honoria?" Ruth asked.

Wiley looked at Fargo, then said, "I think I'll go check on my tent one more time before we go."

He walked off, and Ruth said, "What's the matter with him?"

Fargo grinned. "He didn't want to have to explain to you that Honoria's a scarlet woman."

"And you don't mind telling me?"

"Not a bit. It's not like I'm not doing business with her. But Venus, the scarlet woman I've already told you about, works for her, and Honoria is causing trouble for the marshal. Considering why I'm here, I thought I might give Honoria a little help, seeing as how your brother won't do it."

Ruth shrugged. "It's not really any of my business what Samuel does or doesn't do, and sometimes he can even be wrong. I'll go into town with you, if you don't mind. I thought I'd go by the Cottons' store and look things over."

"I don't blame you," Fargo said. "Let's get you in that buggy you borrowed. Wiley can follow along if he wants to."

"You probably couldn't hold him back," Ruth said.

"That's the truth," Fargo agreed.

Ruth stopped at the store, which happened to be the very one where Fargo had helped the man load his wagon the day before. He hadn't noticed the sign, but he saw it now, COTTON DRY GOODS.

Ruth got out of the buggy and waved to Fargo and Wiley

as they rode on. Wiley said, "You ain't leadin' that little gal on, are you?"

"Me?" Fargo said. "You should know me better than that."

"I know you, all right. That's why I'm askin'." Wiley looked up the street. "What's all that commotion up there? Ain't that Honoria's tent?"

It was, and when they got there they found out what the commotion was all about.

Honoria was dead.

12

Most of the women who'd been employed by Honoria were already long gone. Some had packed whatever possessions they had and moved to some other tent to keep working, while others had started combing the saloons for a place to ply their trade in exchange for a room. And the rest were looking for a way out of town.

One of those who was left was a woman who called herself Pearl. She was sitting at one of the tables in the front of the big tent, drinking Honoria's whiskey with another woman, who said her name was Silver.

"Everybody got out just about as soon as it happened," Pearl told Fargo as she took a healthy gulp of her former employer's liquor. "When somebody dies from something like a curse, you want to get out before your turn comes."

"Not us, though," said Silver, taking down half her glass of whiskey at one swig. "We're not going to let Venus get hanged by that crazy marshal."

Fargo wanted to know what they planned to do, but there was something else he wanted to find out first. He said, "What's that about a curse?"

Pearl looked around as if she thought someone might be listening, though there was no one else in sight.

"You know what I mean," she said.

"No," Fargo said. "I don't have any idea."

"Hell," Wiley said, "that's just because you ain't been here long enough. I told you about it. Ever'body who says anything against the marshal just seems to up and die, mysterious-like. They don't get shot or hung. They just flat-out die. Like Honoria did."

"She must have been sick," Fargo said, knowing better.

Honoria had been about as healthy as anybody he'd seen lately.

"She wasn't sick," Pearl said. "She wasn't sick a day in her life, at least not since I've known her. She felt good all the time. Never even had a runny nose."

"Probably stayed healthy because she drank so much whiskey," Silver said, pouring more into her nearly empty glass.

"Give me some of that," Pearl said. "I need it to get the smell of that old bitch out of my nose."

"What old bitch?" Fargo asked. "Honoria?"

"No," Pearl said. "The marshal's wife. Butter wouldn't melt in her mouth, but she's no better than any of us if the truth were known."

"What does she have to do with this?" Fargo wanted to know.

He was feeling lost. Instead of being enlightened, he was getting more confused. Talking to the two whores made him feel as if he was hearing only half the conversation. He could never quite figure out what they were saying, or what it meant.

"She has a lot to do with it," Silver said, taking the whiskey bottle from Pearl and pouring some more liquor for herself. "She was here this morning, cussing at Honoria, telling her that she'd better quit stirring up trouble if she knew what was good for her."

"Honoria went down to the jail to get the marshal to let Venus go," Pearl said. "We all went with her."

Now she was telling Fargo something that he already knew. He said, "Was there much of an argument between Lattner's wife and Honoria?"

"No. Just a little yelling at first, but they calmed down after that. They even had a drink or two, just to show there were no hard feelings."

"There were hard feelings, though," Silver said. She held her whiskey glass up to the light and gave the amber liquid a thoughtful look. "Anybody could see that, and it don't matter if they had a drink or not. Honoria's still dead."

Fargo didn't believe in curses. If Honoria was dead, it was just a coincidence. Maria couldn't have killed her by yelling at her.

"You talked about doing something to keep the marshal

from hanging Venus," Fargo said. "What did you have planned?"

Pearl gave him a sly look and said, "That's for us to know and you to find out. We're not going to say anything to get ourselves killed like Honoria did. We're way too smart for that."

Fargo wasn't as confident of that as Pearl was, but she didn't notice his skeptical look. She drank from her glass and refused to say anything else, even though Fargo tried to get her to talk. Silver ignored Fargo completely, and after a while he and Wiley gave up trying to get anything more out of the two women.

"If they don't want to tell you, they ain't ever gonna do it," Wiley said, shaking his head as he and Fargo walked away. "People say a whore can't keep a secret, but that's just because they ain't never met any whores. They can keep a secret near about as well as a dead man if they make up their minds to do it."

"Since when did you get to be an expert on whores?" Fargo asked.

"Never you mind about that. I know what I'm talkin' about. What're you gonna do now?"

Fargo said he thought he'd have a talk with Lattner's wife.

"You sure all you're gonna do is talk to her? Maybe you think I don't know what went on yesterday, but I could smell that woman on you from ten feet away. You're likely to wind up like Billy if you don't watch yourself."

Fargo didn't think so, but Pearl and Silver had given him plenty to think about. He said, "You don't have to worry about me. You go on down to the Trail's End and play a few hands of poker. See if you can make some money. I'll talk to Lattner's wife and see what she has to say about Honoria."

Wiley didn't seem to think much of the idea at first, but he gave in after a few seconds.

"I could use a little money," he said. "I need some new supplies, and that reminds me."

"Reminds you of what?"

"That you gotta watch your back here in town. You don't want to get pushed in front of a runaway team again."

"That's not likely to happen," Fargo said.

"Wasn't likely to happen the first time, either. You'd best be careful till that ghost quits hauntin' you."

"It's not a ghost," Fargo said. "But you'd better watch yourself, too. He tore up your camp, and he might decide to tear you up while he's at it."

"He better not mess with me. If he does, we'll see who gets tore up, ghost or no ghost."

Fargo laughed. "You're too tough for him, all right, but be on the lookout anyhow. And try not to lose too much money at that card table."

Wiley was still cussing when Fargo got out of earshot.

Maria was glad to see Fargo, and she ushered him inside. Fargo thought everything would be just fine. But her attitude changed completely when he mentioned Honoria.

"That *puta*," Maria said, without any irony that Fargo could detect. "She was making big trouble for Jack. I told her that she should stop or she would find trouble for herself."

"What did you mean by that?" Fargo asked.

They had moved to the little front room of the marshal's house. Maria had wanted to go in the bedroom but Fargo had told her they needed to talk before they had fun. Judging by the way she was looking at him now, there wasn't much chance they'd be going to the bedroom anytime soon.

"I meant that she would find trouble, just as I said. My husband is a big man in this town, and he won't stand for some whore telling him what to do."

Fargo didn't think this was the right time to bring up the fact that Maria's behavior didn't seem to be much different from that of a whore.

"Your husband's going to hang a woman," Fargo said. "What kind of a man does that?"

"The kind of man who runs his town the way he thinks it ought to be run, without some whores telling him what to do."

"Venus didn't try to tell him what to do."

"You're on her side. I knew it!" Maria clenched her fists and glared at Fargo. Her eyes blazed. "You were with her when she was flaunting herself on the street, trying to make Jack look bad."

"She wasn't flaunting anything, and she wasn't trying to make anybody look bad. She was just trying to be helpful."

"Helpful?" Maria laughed, but there was no humor in it, just bitterness. "I thought you were different, but you're no better than the rest of the men in this town. I'm sure she was very helpful to you, but she won't be helping you again."

Maria stood up, her fists on her hips, her face twisted with anger. Fargo thought she might start throwing things at him at any minute.

"Nobody interferes with my husband's work," she said. "And no one interferes with me. Do you understand what I'm telling you?"

Fargo thought he understood, all right, but not quite as much as he wanted to. But he said, "I take your meaning. I guess I'd better be going."

He stood up, and Maria said, "Yes. Go. That would be for the best. And don't come back."

She slammed the door behind him so hard that Fargo thought the house might fall down. He looked back, and it was still standing, so he started toward the Trail's End to see how Wiley was doing at the poker game.

When Fargo pushed through the batwing doors at the saloon, he saw that the outcome of the poker game had become unimportant. Wiley was in big trouble. Poke Davis was threatening to shoot him.

Davis was standing with his back to the bar and his pistol pointed at Wiley, who stood beside the poker table with his hands raised over his head. There was no one sitting at the table, but there were three men standing nearby. Fargo figured they had been playing cards with Wiley before Davis pulled his pistol.

Davis turned his head slightly when Fargo entered the saloon and smiled when he saw who it was.

"Good to see you, Fargo," he said. "You got here just in time to see me shoot your partner's tallywhacker off."

Wiley looked as if he'd rather die than have that happen. He said, "You do that, and I'll stomp you flat. Not that I'd have to stomp too hard."

Davis gave him a crooked grin. He said, "You'll be sorry you said that, you cheating son of a bitch."

"I never cheated a man in my life," Wiley said. "You ask anybody who was sittin' at the table with me."

The three men who Fargo took for the other gamblers seemed to shrink a little when he said that, and Fargo knew Wiley couldn't count on them to back him up, not as long as Davis had that gun in his hand.

Davis knew it, too. He said, "All right. I'll ask them how they feel. What about it, fellas? Didn't all of you tell me that this dried-up excuse for a card player was cheating you?"

For a second or two nobody said anything. Fargo thought maybe they had spines after all. But they didn't. One of them said, "That's right, Poke. He must've been cheating all along. Otherwise how could he win?"

"You son of a bitch," Wiley said. "I won because you can't play poker any better than you could stop a buffalo stampede with your hat."

"Is that right?" Davis asked, aiming his pistol first at one of the gamblers, then at another.

"No, that's not right," one of them said. His knees were shaking inside his pants. "We all play cards better than he does, but he wins all the time. He's a cheater, all right."

"I reckon he needs hanging then," Davis said. "Or he needs his tallywhacker shot off. Which one do you think it should be, Fargo?"

"Neither one," Fargo said. "Wiley Rawlings never cheated a man in his life, and those tinhorns know it. You know it, too."

"I don't know any such thing," Davis said. "All I know is, he was cheating those fellas, and now he's got to pay for it."

"I don't see it that way," Fargo said.

"You plan to do anything about it?"

"Yes," Fargo said. "I guess I do."

"What would that be?"

"This," Fargo said, and went for his gun.

13

As Fargo drew the big Colt, he dived to his left. He landed on his shoulder and rolled, came up in a crouch, and leveled the gun at the place where Davis had been standing.

But the deputy was no longer there. All over the saloon glasses crashed to the floor and poker chips scattered as men overturned tables to hide behind them or dived beneath them for cover.

The only person who hadn't moved was Wiley, who stood right where he had been. He lowered his hands and looked over at Fargo.

"That was a pretty slick move," he said.

"Where the hell did Davis go?" Fargo asked

"Behind the bar. Damn if I don't think he's near about as fast as you are. He can jump like a damn rabbit, too. By the time you hit the floor he was on top of the bar, and he was down behind it before you were up. It was a sight to see."

"I'm glad you enjoyed it. Why don't you carry a gun?"

"You carry one of them things, and sooner or later you're gonna have to use it. I couldn't hit the side of a mountain if I was standin' next to it, so I figger it's dangerous for me to even own a pistol, much less carry one. Now a rifle's a different thing. I'm a pretty good rifle shot, if I do say so myself. I remember one time—"

"Never mind," Fargo said. "I'm sorry I asked."

The bartender, who'd been standing behind the bar listening to the exchange, eased toward the end of the bar with a frightened look on his face.

"Davis still back there?" Fargo asked him.

The bartender nodded. "Nowhere else for him to go."

"I guess he's still got his pistol."

The bartender nodded again and took another step backward. He stood still for a second or two, then moved aside quickly. Davis stuck his head around the end of the bar like a rat sneaking a look from a hole in the wall.

Fargo snapped off a quick shot, tearing a chunk of wood off the end of the bar. The bullet whined off and hit the wall, missing Davis, who had pulled back.

The bartender hopped aside again, and Fargo figured that Davis was heading for the other end of the bar. He got ready to shoot, but Davis had other plans. He jumped up and appeared on the middle of the bar, standing up solid and real as if he'd been conjured by a magician. He got off one shot before Fargo even knew he was there. The bullet tore into the floor and plowed up a short furrow near Fargo's left boot.

Fargo fired back, but by then Davis was gone. Fargo's shot smashed a whiskey bottle, sending whiskey and shards of glass flying. One piece of glass hit the bartender under one eye. The bartender yelled. Blood welled out of his cheek, and he raised his hand to wipe it off.

"Agile little fart, ain't he?" Wiley said. "Jumps around like a damn jackass rabbit."

There was another shot, and a hole appeared in the back of the bartender's hand. The bullet went right on through the palm and hit the bartender in the face, taking half of the man's jaw away. The bartender fell heavily forward and disappeared behind the bar. Gunsmoke swirled up and curled away.

"Son of a bitch don't much care who he kills, does he?" Wiley said. "Course he don't have to worry, bein' as how he's a deputy and all. Nobody's gonna come lookin' for him to string him up."

Davis's head appeared over the top of the bar, and he fired a shot at Wiley, whose hat flew off and flipped over twice before hitting the wall. Wiley, evidently deciding that standing up was getting to be a little too dangerous, dropped down behind one of the overturned tables.

Fargo fired back at the deputy, but Davis ducked behind the bar, and all Fargo's bullet did was shatter another bottle of whiskey.

"Little bastard was standin' on the bartender," Wiley

called out to Fargo. "What kind of a man'd use a dead man for a footstool?"

"A short one," Fargo said, wondering if the dwarf might be reloading. "What started all this, anyway?"

"You did," Wiley said. "Davis come in here, and when he saw me, he asked where you were. I said I didn't know, and he called me a liar. When that didn't get a rise out of me, he called me a cheat."

"And that got a rise out of you?" Fargo said.

"Hell, no. But then he shot a hole in the wall over there and that pretty much got a rise out of ever'body here. When he had our attention, he said he was gonna shoot my tallywhacker off if I didn't tell him where you were."

"But you didn't tell him."

"Nope. But only because you come walkin' in through the door. Otherwise, I would've told him quick. I'd a whole lot rather have him out huntin' you down than get my tallywhacker shot off. He might not've been able to find you if he went lookin', and I'm kinda partial to that little pecker of mine."

Fargo couldn't really blame Wiley for that. He said, "You still down behind that bar, Davis?"

There was no answer, but then Fargo hadn't really expected one. Davis wouldn't want Fargo to know exactly where he was.

"How long you reckon he can lurk around back there?" Wiley asked.

Fargo didn't know the answer to that one, but he was sure of one thing. By now somebody had almost certainly told the marshal about all the shooting in the saloon, and Lattner was probably on the way there. If he wasn't already, he soon would be.

Fargo decided that it was time to leave. He motioned for Wiley to follow him and started backing toward the door.

It was as if Davis had sensed what Fargo was going to do. He jumped upon the bar again, shooting twice in rapid succession. A hot wind ripped past Fargo's face, and something tugged at his sleeve. Fargo didn't let it bother him. He shot the dwarf squarely in middle of his chest.

Davis flew back off the bar and crashed into the bottles behind it. He hung there for just a second, suspended against the cracked mirror, before falling to the floor. Shattered bottles fell atop the dwarf's body, and whiskey ran all over the floor.

"I hate to see good liquor wasted like that," Wiley said, standing up. "But I'm glad to see that son of a bitch dead. I don't think the marshal's gonna feel the same way about it, though. He really liked that little sawed-off bastard."

"It'd be just as well if he didn't find us here, then," Fargo said. "Come on."

They went outside, leaving everyone else still crouched around the place, afraid to show their faces. There was a crowd outside standing around the door, but Fargo pushed through them. People were shouting questions at him. Fargo ignored them.

"Too bad we left our horses down by the jail," Wiley said. "But then maybe it's time you and Lattner had it out."

Fargo was thinking the same thing. Devil's Creek was the craziest town he'd ever been in, and he was ready to shake the dust of its streets off his feet and get out. He'd come there to see what he could do about Billy Banks being hanged, but he hadn't wanted to force the issue. Now Davis had taken care of that for him.

The whole mess was very unsatisfying, however. Fargo still didn't know the real reason Billy had been hanged, although it didn't appear that Lattner or his deputy needed a reason for killing people. Nothing in the whole damned town made any sense as far as Fargo could tell. There were a couple of things nagging at the back of Fargo's mind, however—things he thought might help him put everything in some kind of order if only he could sort them out—but he didn't have time to worry about that now.

He and Wiley walked all the way to the jail without seeing Lattner. When they got there, they went inside. There was a man sitting in the office. He was tipped back in the chair, his feet propped up on the desk, and he was holding a shotgun across his lap.

"Howdy, Wiley," he said, putting a hand on the gun and aiming it in Wiley's general direction. With a gun like that, a general direction was all you needed. "I hope you're not here to make trouble about that little whore we got back in the cells. I'd hate to have to shoot you and your friend."

"My friend's name is Skye Fargo," Wiley said. "Not that

you'd hate shootin' anybody. Fargo, this here's Frank Delong. He's another one of Lattner's deputies. Not quite as bad as Davis, though."

"Mighty nice of you to say so," Delong told him. "You two the cause of all the ruckus down at the Trail's End?"

"What ruckus?" Wiley asked. "I didn't hear about any ruckus."

"Somebody came down here looking for the marshal," Delong said. "Told me there was a big gunfight going on at the saloon."

"Wouldn't know," Wiley said. "I don't carry a gun, myself. Where's the marshal, anyhow?"

"Don't know," Delong said. "Might be at his house. He's been a little under the weather today. Left me here on guard. He figured somebody might try to break that little whore out, maybe by causing some kind of trouble to distract me. Told me not to leave here under any circumstances. So here I sit."

"I like a fella who knows his duty," Wiley said. "That mean you're not gonna check out the ruckus?"

"Nope. That's the marshal's job. He told me to guard the whore, and that's what I'm doing."

"Well, if you do see Lattner, tell him we came by looking for him," Fargo said.

"I'll be sure to do that. Where can he find you?"

"He won't have to find us," Fargo said. "We'll find him." Delong nodded and said, "I'll be sure to let him know." Fargo nodded, and he and Wiley left.

"You really gonna go lookin' for him?" Wiley asked.

"Damn right," Fargo said.

They looked all over town, but they didn't find Lattner. They started at his house. Fargo thought he saw someone moving around inside, but no one would come to the door, and Fargo didn't want to break in.

After that, they went back to the Trail's End. The place still smelled of gunsmoke and whiskey, but Davis and the bartender were gone.

Silver was there, however, sitting at a table by herself and looking dejected. She told Fargo that the town's undertaker had come for the bodies and with the help of several of the men had carted them away.

"From what I hear, which isn't much," she said, "you two are the ones responsible for this mess. They say Fargo killed Davis, and the bartender, too."

"I didn't kill the bartender," Fargo said. "Davis did that."

"Try to make those folks believe it," Silver said, nodding toward the other occupants of the room, none of whom would look in her direction, probably because she was talking to Fargo.

"You two have pretty much messed up my chances of picking up any business here," she said. "I thought I might make a dollar or two this afternoon, but now I'll be lucky to get a free drink."

Fargo saw what she meant. The men in the saloon sat in tight little groups, talking quietly, and nobody wanted to look up and meet Fargo's gaze.

"You can always go drink a little more of Honoria's whiskey," he said.

"Good idea," Silver said. "You want to walk me down the street?"

"Now, that wouldn't be a good idea. You know what happened to Venus."

"So you're the one who caused it. I should've known."

"Known what?"

"That Lattner bitch was jealous. She's the one who got the marshal to arrest Venus."

"I don't know what you're talking about," Fargo said.

"Sure you do. A man like you doesn't have to find him a whore. He can always find a woman who'll spread her legs for him and not charge him a dime. Not that it makes you special where Maria Lattner is concerned. She's spread her legs for more than one man in this town. All of them are dead now, though."

"One of 'em damn sure is," Wiley said. "Name of Billy Banks."

"He was one of them," Silver said. "Not the only one. I could name a few others."

"Maybe we'll walk you back to that whiskey bottle, after all," Fargo said, extending his arm.

"The hell you will. Now that I know why Venus is in jail getting ready to hang, I wouldn't walk to the door with you, much less show myself on the street."

"Sorry to hear you feel that way," Fargo said. "Because I really do need to talk to you. You don't have to worry about the marshal's wife doing anything. We aren't exactly on speaking terms."

Silver looked around. Nobody would look their way.

"You never know when one of those yellow skunks'll tell on you," she said. "And it don't matter whether you're friends with her or not, considering the fix Venus is in. But if we make it look like business, maybe people will keep their mouths shut. We can go to a room, but you'll have to pay."

Fargo agreed, and Silver started toward the rear of the saloon.

"There's a couple of rooms back here," she said. Seeing that Wiley was coming along after them, she added, "You can stay right where you are, you old coot. This is between me and your big friend."

"Dammit," Wiley said, "I never get in on any of the fun."

"This isn't fun," Fargo told him. "It's business."

"It better be. I don't like the idea of you goin' off with a woman all by yourself. I know what you're like."

Fargo didn't say anything to that. He followed Silver on to the back of the saloon and into one of the rooms there.

"What will the owner think about this?" he asked when she had closed the door.

"Not much," she said. "In fact, he won't be thinking about anything again. He was the bartender."

"Who'll take over here?"

"I don't know," Silver said. "And I don't care."

"Could it be the marshal?"

"Could be. So what?"

"Just wondering," Fargo said, thinking that Davis may have had saloon ownership on his mind when he killed the owner. Or maybe Davis just liked to shoot people.

"You know that the marshal put a lot of stock in that little deputy of his," Silver said. "Poke was like his lucky piece."

"So I've heard."

"That means he's going to hang you or kill you as soon as he gets a chance."

"I might be more worried about that if he was around.

As it is, he's dropped off the face of the earth. Besides, I shot Davis in self-defense."

Silver laughed. "I guess you think that makes a difference. You saw what it was like out there. Nobody's going to vouch for you. They've already got you killing the bartender, too."

Fargo knew she was right. Lattner would be gunning for him, but he didn't care about that. Once the confrontation was over, Fargo would have done what he came to Devil's Creek to do, even if he didn't know the answers to all his questions. And that thought reminded him of what he'd come to the room to ask Silver about.

"You said something about Maria Lattner spreading her legs for a lot of other men and that they were all dead."

Silver nodded and said, "I told you that you were going to have to pay if you came in here with me, too."

Fargo gave her the money. He said, "Now start talking."

Silver tucked the money away in the bosom of her dress and told him what she knew.

14

"You mean to tell me," Wiley said, "that all those men who got hung were messin' around with Maria Lattner?"

"That's what Silver claims," Fargo said.

He and Wiley were on their way back to Wiley's place. They'd stopped in at the jail again, and Lattner was still gone. Delong was there, with his shotgun, but he didn't have anything else to add to what he'd already told them.

"That's a lot of men," Wiley said. "Too bad Billy had to be one of 'em. I guess Lattner must be the jealous type."

Fargo shook his head and said, "That's not it. It has something to do with his idea that he's here to cleanse the world of sinners, and fornication being one of the worst sins, he just naturally has to get rid of fornicators."

"Does fornicatin' mean what I think it does?"

"I expect so."

"Then why hasn't he hung his wife? Seems to me she must be the worst fornicator in town."

It seemed that way to Fargo, too. He said, "He doesn't seem to think his wife can do any wrong. She's got the wool pulled over his eyes."

"She's pulled her wool over a lot of eyes, to hear your friend Silver tell it."

"I didn't mean it like that," Fargo said, laughing.

"Comes to about the same thing. You want to know what's worryin' me now?"

Fargo said he reckoned he did.

"What worries me is that dead dwarf. What if he comes back to life and gets after you like that other man you killed?"

Fargo had momentarily forgotten about Tom. There hadn't been any sign of him all day.

"Maybe he's given up," Fargo said. "He's found out I'm too hard for him to kill."

"I wouldn't count on that if I was you. A ghost don't give up that easy."

"Everybody gives up, sooner or later," Fargo said.

"What about you? Would you give up if you was out to get somebody?"

Fargo thought briefly about the men who'd killed his family. He knew he'd never give up on those bastards.

"No," he said. "I wouldn't."

"Didn't think so. I'll bet you this Tom fella is the same way, and I know for sure Lattner is. I wonder what the hell's happened to him."

Fargo wondered the same thing, but he couldn't quite figure it out.

"Besides those two, we got us another little problem," Wiley said.

"Just what we need," Fargo said.

"If we don't do something, Lattner's gonna hang that little whore tomorrow."

"I know that," Fargo said.

"Well, what're we gonna do about it?"

Fargo didn't have an answer.

"You reckon those whores are gonna do anything like they said?"

"What could they do? There are only two of them. That was the whiskey talking."

"You never know about whores," Wiley said. "Sometimes they can fool you."

"You're the expert," Fargo told him.

It was getting along toward late afternoon when they got back to Wiley's camp. The sun was going down behind the Bitterroots, lighting their snowy tops like candles. The lower slopes were already dark. Around Wiley's camp the tops of the pines were bright green in the last rays of the sun.

"I'll rustle us up something to eat," Wiley said, "if you'll see to the horses."

Fargo was taking care of that chore when Ruth rode up.

Fargo was surprised to see her. He'd thought when she told him about her brother's matchmaking that she wouldn't be paying any more visits to him. But she wasn't there to socialize.

"There's trouble in town, Fargo," she said. "I was about to leave the Cottons' store when it started. You seem to have some sympathy for that woman in the jail, and if you do, you'd better get to town right now."

Fargo put the saddle back on his Ovaro and asked what was going on.

"There are some women causing trouble," Ruth told him.

Fargo didn't have to ask which women. Silver and Pearl had told him they had something in mind, though they hadn't told him what. If they'd continued drinking Honoria's whiskey all afternoon, there was no telling what they might be up to.

"Have you told Samuel?" he asked Ruth.

"I thought I'd better let you know first."

Fargo didn't have to ask why. Samuel might have been a preacher, but his sense of Christian charity didn't seem to extend to whores.

"You go tell him what's going on," Fargo said, tightening the cinch girth. "He's a lot more likely to be able to calm things down than we are."

"I'd rather go back to town with you," Ruth said.

"I don't think that would be a good idea. Wiley and I will do what we can, but the marshal might try to lock us up with Venus. What are those women doing?"

Ruth blushed and looked down at the ground.

"They're parading around in next to nothing. They say they're going to take all their clothes off if the marshal doesn't let their friend go."

They'd been drinking all afternoon, all right, Fargo thought. They'd have to be pretty drunk to come up with an idea like that, but it seemed harmless enough. He called Wiley over and told him what was going on.

"That sounds like a sight to see," Wiley said with a grin. "I'm ready to go if you are."

"It's not as funny as it sounds," Ruth said. "I'm afraid that the marshal is going to try to arrest them. They're not going to cooperate if he does, and somebody's going to get hurt. There was a crowd gathering even before I left."

"I bet there was," Wiley said. "Come on, Fargo, let's go see for ourselves."

Fargo climbed on the Ovaro's back and told Ruth again to fetch Samuel. Then he and Wiley headed back into town.

It didn't take them long, and when they arrived at the jail, the moon was rising in the black night sky. The people in the crowd looked spectrally pale in its light, and the moon cast the shadow of the nearby gallows over some of the men standing at the edge of the group. Several of the men were carrying lanterns, which added their own eerie glow to the scene.

Sitting on the Ovaro, Fargo could see over the heads of the people gathered in the street. Delong was standing in the doorway of the jail, holding his shotgun. There was no sign of Lattner that Fargo could see, and he wondered again where the marshal was. He seemed to have disappeared completely from the town. It was almost as if he'd never been there.

Up in the front of the crowd, near the jail, were Silver and Pearl. Ruth had described their clothing fairly accurately, Fargo thought, or what there was left of it. The outlines of their firm breasts and rounded hips showed clearly through the thin garments, and while most of the men in the crowd seemed quite happy to be there, the few women were not. They were whispering to the men and pulling on their arms, trying to get them to leave. But the men weren't budging.

Silver was saying something to Delong, and Fargo strained to hear over the buzz of the crowd.

"You can't keep Venus locked up in there any longer," Silver said. "If you do, Pearl and I will take our clothes off right here in the street. Then you'll have to try to arrest us, but you can't. If you try, we'll run. And then what'll you do?"

Fargo could see that Delong was a man in a quandary. He couldn't fire the shotgun because he might hit some of the men or women in the crowd. That probably wouldn't have bothered either Davis or Lattner, but Delong appeared to be more sensible than those two. He must have known that if he hurt someone, the crowd might suddenly turn on him. He'd have only one shot left, and he could never stop all of them if they stormed the jail.

Delong looked out over the crowd as if hoping to avoid saying anything to the two women, and Fargo caught his eye.

"Why don't you just let the woman go?" Fargo called out. "She hasn't done anything but try to earn a living."

People looked around to see who was doing the talking. One of the men, obviously a miner, shouted out his agreement.

"She's just trying to make a living," he said. "This town needs more like her, not less. Let her go!"

Several of the miners cheered and waved their hats above their heads. A couple of women tried to pull their arms down but succeeded only in making their gesturing more fervent.

Silver and Pearl were encouraged. They started moving around, pulling at their skimpy garments as if intending to tear them off. The men in the front of the crowd howled encouragement. One man off to the side set down his lantern, and he and the man next to him started a clumsy dance. Puffs of dust rose from the street while a couple of other men clapped their hands to keep time.

Silver pulled up the long skirt of her outfit and showed off her calves. The men howled louder. One of the women turned around with a disgusted look on her face and walked away. Fargo wondered just how far Silver would go.

"I can't find Samuel," Ruth said at Fargo's side.

He'd been so caught up in the little drama unfolding in front of him that he hadn't even heard her ride up.

"Someone has to do something," Ruth went on. "This could get dangerous."

Fargo knew she was right, but he didn't know what to do. Besides, he believed that Silver and Pearl were right. Venus should be released from the jail, and she certainly shouldn't hang for something that Fargo didn't really consider a crime.

"You turn Venus loose," Pearl said, standing with her arms akimbo, "and we'll all go away and leave you alone."

The crowd got quiet for a second. Delong looked as if he wanted to do what Pearl said, but he was too scared of what Lattner might do to him if he went through with it.

The two miners who had been dancing stopped, and one of them shouted, "By God, I don't see why you can't just let that little gal go. If Lattner gives you any trouble, just tell him to go to hell."

"That's right," another man cried. "Tell him to go to hell."

"I can't do that," Delong said. "I'm the law here. You people need to go on home and let the law take care of things."

"That's what we've been doin' for too damn long," Wiley called out, to Fargo's surprise.

Fargo turned his head to look at his friend. Wiley shrugged his shoulders and gave him a crooked grin.

"That's right," a man yelled. "We've been letting Jack Lattner take care of us, and he's hung half the town. Are we gonna let him hang a woman now, or are we gonna do something about it?"

"We're gonna do something," one of the dancers said.

He reached down and picked up his lantern by the wire bail, and before Delong could do anything to stop him, he hurled it atop the jail. The glass shattered and coal oil leaked out of the metal bottom, catching fire almost immediately.

A cheer went up from the crowd, and two more men threw their lanterns onto the roof. The blaze quickly spread across half the wooden surface, and the smell of smoke and burning wood filled the street. The crowd backed away from the jail, leaving Delong standing in the doorway with Pearl and Silver in front of him. The two women looked up at the burning roof and then at each other.

"Venus is in there," Pearl said to Delong. "You got to get her out right now, before she burns up."

Delong smiled and said, "The hell I do. You didn't want her to get hanged, and it looks like you'll get your wish. But she's not gonna like what happens to her now any better than she would hanging. In fact, I'd say she's gonna feel a lot worse about it before it's all over."

Silver took a step toward him, and he pointed the shotgun at her stomach.

"You come a little closer," he said, "and there won't be any spread to the shot. It'll cut you right in two."

"You wouldn't do that," Wiley said. "I know you better than that, Delong."

Delong looked out over the crowd until he saw Wiley.

"You don't know me a-tall, Wiley Rawlings," he said. "Marshal Lattner set me to do a job, and I'm doing it the best way I know how. If anybody wants to get shot, then let 'em come on. I'm just the man can do the job."

"He can't just let the jail burn down around him," Ruth said to Fargo.

"Yes, he can," Wiley said. "He don't care a whit about that gal in there. He's a hell of a lot more worried about what Lattner'll do to him if he lets her loose than he is about anything else."

It hadn't rained for a while in Devil's Creek, and the wood of the jail was dry. The fire was spreading rapidly. Fargo could hear the crackling of the flames. It was time to make a move.

He put his heels to the Ovaro's sides and rode straight through the crowd. The men who didn't move out of the way got knocked down or shoved aside by the big horse.

Delong saw Fargo coming and raised the shotgun higher, but he hesitated for just a fraction of a second, which was a fraction too long. Fargo drew and shot him before he could pull the trigger.

The deputy fell in the doorway, dropping the shotgun. Silver ran to where it lay and grabbed it up. Fargo had shot Delong through the shoulder, and the deputy kicked his legs, squirming around and trying to get up. Silver held the shotgun awkwardly and pointed it in the approximate direction of his head.

"Just lie right there, still and quiet," she said.

Delong looked up at her. Whatever he saw in her eyes must have convinced him that she'd shoot. He sighed and lay back.

Fargo slid off his horse and pushed through the jail door. The office inside was already filled with smoke, and parts of the roof were burning through. Fargo couldn't see a thing. He went back outside.

"Where are the keys to the cells?" he asked Delong.

"You go to hell," the deputy said.

"You're the one going to hell if you don't tell him," Silver said. She put the barrel of the shotgun solidly against his forehead. "So tell him, you son of a bitch."

"The sheriff has a set," Delong said. "He keeps 'em with him all the time."

Silver ground the shotgun into Delong's skin.

"There's a set hanging by the door to the cells," Delong said. "Right-hand side."

Fargo took a deep breath of the night air and went back inside. He couldn't see where he was going, so he just walked in as straight a line as he could toward the back of the office where he remembered the cell door was located. He walked into a chair and barked his shins. He shoved the chair out of his way and kept moving. Then he was at the wall.

He felt his way to the door and fumbled around until he found the keys. It took him three tries to find the one that fit the door. By that time he had to take a breath. The smoke was burning his eyes, and he made the breath a shallow one. Even at that, he took in some smoke.

Throwing open the door, Fargo stopped just long enough to tie his bandana over his nose and mouth. When he was finished, he said, "Venus, it's Skye Fargo. Where are you?"

"Right here," she said. "In the first cell."

Fargo felt the bars to his right. They were already getting quite warm. He located the lock. This time it took him only two tries to find the key that fit. He turned it and swung the door open.

Just as he did, a big chunk of the roof caved in. Fargo had to jump into the cell to avoid it. When he did that, he knocked Venus down. She lay on the floor, coughing. Sparks and fiery cinders drifted toward them.

Fargo reached down and found Venus's arm. He dragged her to her feet.

"Come on along," he said. "We're getting out of here."

He moved out of the cell, pulling Venus along after him. She didn't say anything, but he could hear her coughing. Most of the roof was on fire by that time, and the heat seared the exposed areas of Fargo's face.

Outside there was shouting and shooting. Fargo didn't know what was going on, but there was clearly some kind of excitement that seemed unrelated to the jail fire. He didn't know what kind of fire wagon the town had, or even if it had one. If it did, there had been no sign of it. No one was coming to his rescue.

The flames crackled on the roof. They had begun to spread to the walls as well.

Fargo looked for the outline of the outside doorway and saw it across the smoky room.

When he started moving toward the doorway, pulling Venus along, a dark shape blocked the dim light.

It looked like a big man wearing a buffalo robe.

15

Fargo had a strong feeling that the man in the robe hadn't come to help him.

He was right. The man moved toward him purposefully, as if he could see clearly though the smoke.

Fargo pulled Venus close and asked, "Can you see the door?"

Venus answered with a cough. She caught her breath and said, "Yes."

"Then run for it," Fargo said, "and don't run into anybody."

He pushed her in the direction of the indistinct rectangle, and she stumbled away from him, dodging past the big man who blocked her path. He made no move to stop her. It was clear that he wasn't there for her. It was Fargo he wanted.

Part of a rafter fell on top of the sheriff's desk and shattered into coals. In the brief flare of light that it provided, Fargo saw Venus disappear through the door. The man in the robe was wearing a hat pulled low over his eyes. Fargo tried to see his face, but there was nothing but shadow.

The man stood still as a stone for a second or two. Then he launched himself at Fargo.

Fargo was braced and ready, but the man hit him so hard that Fargo was carried backward several steps, almost to the door leading to the cell block. The air was knocked from his lungs, and he was forced to take a breath of air mixed with the thick smoke. His lungs burned, and his eyes teared, but he managed to free himself from the man and to pull his gun.

The big man knocked the gun aside and slammed a fist

into Fargo's face. Fargo fell, dropping the pistol and staggering into the cell block.

The robed man followed, taking advantage of Fargo's lack of equilibrium to shove him into the cell that Venus had just vacated. Fargo fell back against the wall and slumped to the floor as the cell door slammed shut. A key turned in the lock.

The man stood for a second staring through the bars, then turned and walked away, disappearing into the smoke.

Fargo shook his head to clear it, but shaking didn't help. The smoke burned his eyes and blurred his vision. It clogged his throat and made breathing nearly impossible. The bandana wasn't helping much.

Fargo went to the cell door. It was locked tightly. He could hardly even rattle the rapidly heating bars. Then Fargo remembered something: he had a set of keys, too.

Fargo fumbled at the waistband of his pants. The keys were hanging from a large ring, and the ring was stuck behind Fargo's gunbelt. He pulled them out and started fitting them into the door, trying not to hurry, even though he was sure the whole roof might fall on him at any second. Or the walls might topple in, bringing the whole jail down. If that happened, there wasn't likely to be much more left of Fargo than a crisp burned husk.

His fingers were clumsy, but he separated the keys and tried one.

It didn't work. Neither did the second, nor the third. Fargo wondered if he was doing something wrong, but the fourth key turned in the lock, and the door swung open. Fargo left, taking the keys with him. You never could tell when they might come in handy.

As he shuffled through the sheriff's office, he kicked something hard that lay on the floor. Reaching down, he picked up his pistol and stuck it in the holster.

As he was rising, someone grabbed his arm. Fargo jerked out the pistol and stuck it in the side of the man holding him.

"Goddamn!" Wiley said. "What the hell's wrong with you, Fargo? I come in here to save your scrawny ass, and you pull a gun on me."

"Sorry," Fargo said, his voice roughed by the smoke he'd inhaled. "Let's get out of here."

When they were outside and well away from the jail, Fargo saw that the gallows was also on fire. The entire crowd stood around it, watching it as it slowly toppled over. When it fell, the people let out a cheer. At about the same time, the walls of the jail fell in with a crash, sending sparks and flame high into the air.

"That's the end of that," Wiley said.

"They can build another one," Fargo said, but he figured he wouldn't be needing those keys again after all. "Did you see the man who came in there after me?"

Wiley shook his head. "Wasn't nobody in there but me."

"What about Venus?"

"Didn't see her, either. When you went in there after her, Ruth and me got down off our horses to come get you, but about that time somebody set the gallows on fire. Ruth and me got carried over that way by the mob, and by the time I got myself shook loose, the jail was just about burned down. But I figgered you were still in there, so I went after you, riskin' life and limb to see if you'd got out yet. And what do I get? A gun stuck in my gut, that's what."

"I thought you were someone else."

"And who the hell could I have been? Like I said, there wasn't anybody in there but you and me."

"There was someone in there with me before you came," Fargo said. "The man in the buffalo robe. He locked me in a cell."

"You right sure about that?" Wiley asked. "I didn't see nobody go in or out of there."

"You were busy. He was there all right."

"Proves he's a ghost, then. No live man could get in and out of there and lock you up and then just disappear. Not that I'm doubtin' your word, but if you were locked in a cell, how'd you get out?"

Fargo held up the keys and jangled them in front of Wiley's face.

"Pretty smart of you to have those things with you," Wiley said.

Fargo didn't comment. He looked around the crowd, searching for the man in the robe. There was no sign him, but he did see Ruth coming toward them.

"Speakin' of Venus," Wiley said, "you didn't leave her

in there, did you? 'Cause if you did, she's gonna be pretty well cooked by now."

"She's not in there."

"Ghost get her?"

"There's not any ghost," Fargo said, "and he didn't get her, not as far as I know."

Ruth reached them at that point and asked what he meant about the ghost. Fargo told her what had happened.

"You look like you're about half a ghost, yourself," she said when he was finished. "You must have nearly died in there. Was it Tom who locked you in?"

Fargo said he didn't know. It didn't seem very likely that it could have been Tom, but then nothing about Devil's Creek was likely. Including the fact that the marshal hadn't showed up for the burning of his own jail.

And that thought reminded Fargo of Delong. He asked Wiley what had happened to him.

"They drug him over there to string him up," Wiley said. "They decided they'd give him a little necktie party, but then somebody set the gallows on fire instead. I guess Delong's just as glad about that. He's lyin' over there in the street somewhere."

Fargo didn't much care, really. He wanted to find Venus, and he wanted to find Tom, or whoever the robed man was.

But the robed man was gone, and so was Venus. There was no sign of either one of them anywhere. Fargo made his way through the mob in front of the gallows to where Silver and Pearl were standing.

"I got Venus out of the jail," he said.

"I knew you would," Pearl said.

She reached up and wiped some soot off Fargo's forehead.

"You're the only one who had the nerve to go in there after her," Silver said. "If you ever want a sample of the merchandise, you can ask for me or Pearl. No charge."

Fargo thanked her, but he wasn't in the mood right at the moment.

"Where is Venus?" Pearl said. "If you got her out, she ought to be here."

"That's who I'm looking for," Fargo said. "Someone else came in the jail and caused me a little trouble, so Venus got out before I did. I haven't been able to find her."

"Maybe she went back to Honoria's place," Pearl said.

Fargo followed Pearl and Silver, with Ruth and Wiley coming along behind. Ruth wasn't so sure she wanted to go along, however.

"What will Samuel say if he finds out I've been associating with scarlet women?" she asked.

Fargo didn't answer, but judging from the things Samuel had said previously, he wouldn't be too happy about it.

Wiley, however, wasn't worried. He said, "Bein' a preacher, your brother's bound to know that story about castin' the first stone. He won't say anything as long as you don't get any ideas about finding yourself a new line of work."

"Mr. Cotton might not like it either," Ruth said, and Wiley wanted to know what the Cottons had to do with it.

Ruth explained, and Wiley said, "That Bob Cotton is a nice enough young fella, and if he likes you, you could do worse. But he won't say a thing about you visitin' Honoria's place if he has any sense. He's been there more'n once, himself."

Ruth laughed, and Wiley apologized. "I didn't mean to be sayin' anything bad about him. You can bet he wouldn't want his mama to know he'd been there, or his intended, either. I guess I just got a big mouth."

"Don't worry about it," Ruth said. "It's always good for a woman to know things like that."

"Yeah, so she can marry some fella and lead him a merry chase," Wiley said. "I reckon that's why I never got married. I never liked for anybody to have the upper hand on me."

Ruth laughed again. "I can see there's not much danger of that happening," she said.

"Dadgum right," Wiley told her.

When they reached Honoria's tent, there was no one there. If Venus had been there after escaping from the jail, there was no evidence of it.

"I think most of the girls will come back by tomorrow," Silver said. "Once they see what's happened to the jail."

"And Delong won't be botherin' anybody for a while," Wiley said. "They won't have to worry about him, either. You gals can start the business right up again."

"What about Jack Lattner?" Pearl said. "Has anybody seen him?"

Fargo told her that nobody had.

"He won't settle for letting us open again," Silver said. "Not after all that's happened. He'll want to get Venus again, if she comes back."

"Maybe she'll turn up tomorrow," Fargo said.

"That might not be smart," Silver said. "Lattner might just arrest her again. He wouldn't need a gallows to hang her from. He could just use a cottonwood tree."

Fargo wasn't as worried about Lattner as he was about the man in the robe, but he didn't say that. Silver and Pearl wouldn't have known what he was talking about.

"I'll look for Venus for a while longer," Fargo said. "If I can find her, she can stay with me and Wiley for a while."

Silver and Pearl seemed to think that was a good idea, and Wiley said he thought it was a fine idea.

"Don't go getting any ideas," Fargo said.

"Me?" Wiley said. "You know me better'n that, Fargo. I ain much on ideas. I just want her to have a place to stay."

Fargo said he didn't doubt it. "Let's go find our horses and see if we can locate Venus."

Ruth and Wiley agreed that was the thing to do, and they started back toward the jail.

"You know what I'm thinkin'?" Wiley said after they'd walked a short distance. "I'm thinking that damn ghost has got Venus."

Fargo nodded. He'd been thinking exactly the same thing.

16

When they got to what was left of the jail, most of the crowd had left. There were only a few people standing around, and none of them admitted to having seen either Venus or the big man in the buffalo robe.

Had the man been Jack Lattner? He had the keys to the cells, but he wasn't exactly the right size. It was something Fargo would have to think about.

Delong was gone, too. Fargo asked where he was, and a man told him that the deputy had managed to leave on his own.

"He wasn't hurt all that bad," the man said. "Just shot through the shoulder."

Fargo, being the one who'd shot him, knew that. He wondered if Delong had gone to find Lattner, but no one knew.

The jail and the gallows were nothing more than smoldering piles of charred wood, which Fargo thought was all for the best. Maybe Lattner, if he came back from wherever he was, wouldn't be so quick to hang people.

"What with that ghost wanderin' around," Wiley said, "we better ride to the Cottons with Ruth to make sure she gets there."

Fargo thought that was a good idea, and he and Wiley went with her to the Cottons' house before going to Wiley's camp.

"This is all mighty strange," Wiley said. "People disappearin', ghosts showing up out of nowhere. When I asked you to come here, I never thought it would get this complicated."

"Me neither," Fargo said.

*   *   *

The next morning, Fargo was sore all over. His throat was raw, and his eyes were red. He smelled like he'd been roasted over an open fire.

"You look like you been struck with the wrath of God," Wiley said when he saw him.

"I feel that way, too," Fargo said, and went to the creek to clean himself up.

He laid his clothes on the bank to air out and went into the water. It was cold, and he thought about the chilly nights that Ruth had warmed up on their way to Devil's Creek. It wasn't likely they'd be doing that again, not with her considering getting married to Bob Cotton.

Fargo tried to relax and let the water soak some of the aches out of his body. He thought over everything that had happened to him since his arrival in Devil's Creek, going over what people had said and done. He couldn't help thinking that there was something he'd overlooked, something that would help him figure out just what was happening. But if there was anything, it didn't come to him.

Clouds were massing behind the Bitterroots, turning the sky purple. Fargo could hear the sound of distant thunder, and now and then a streak of lightning split the clouds. The wind picked up and blew through the trees.

Fargo got dressed and started back to Wiley's camp. On the way, he thought he heard someone calling him from the trees. It was nothing distinct. It was long and drawn out, a whispery kind of voice like a ghost might use.

"Fa-a-a-a-r-r-r-go."

The wind from the mountains rustled through the trees, rasping the leaves of the cottonwoods and stirring the needles of the pines, and at first Fargo thought he might have imagined the voice. But then it came again.

"Fa-a-a-a-r-r-r-go."

He turned to locate the place where the voice was coming from, but it seemed to come from everywhere at once.

"Fa-a-a-a-r-r-r-go."

He wondered for a second or two if Wiley might be playing a trick on him, or if Ruth had come back for one more romp with him before she settled down with the storekeeper. But Fargo knew that wasn't it. There was someone, or something, out there. He drew his pistol and moved into the trees, looking all around to be sure that no one came at him from behind.

As he got farther into the trees, the voice faded and died away on the wind. Fargo stood and listened, but now the only whispering he heard was the stirring of the leaves. He was about to turn back when he saw something moving back in the trees. He went forward cautiously, and before long he came to a tall cottonwood.

Venus was hanging from one of its branches.

Her face was mottled and scratched, and Fargo could hardly see the thin line of the scar that marked her. Her tongue protruded from her mouth, and her feet dangled down several feet above the ground. Fargo walked to the body and touched it. It was stiff and cold, and Fargo knew that Venus had been hanged there hours earlier, probably the previous night.

On the ground there were indistinct hoofprints. Tom, the ghost, or whoever it was, had brought Venus there on horseback, tossed the rope over the tree limb, and put the noose over her neck. Then he'd ridden over to the tree and tied the end of the rope around the trunk.

Fargo imagined Venus hanging from the limb, kicking and clawing at the rope around her neck. She hadn't deserved to die like that. Fargo hoped she hadn't lasted very long.

He was about to turn away when he noticed something on the tightly stretched length of rope that ran to the tree. He walked over to have a look. It was soot, and Fargo touched his fingers to it. He was sure it was burned hair from a buffalo robe.

Thunder boomed overhead, and rain rattled down through the trees.

Despite the rain, Fargo spent some time looking around in the woods, but he couldn't find the man in the robe. Any tracks other than the ones he'd seen right around the tree were washed away. The rain was cold, and soaked into Fargo's buckskins. He figured it was at least getting rid of the rest of the smoke smell.

After spending several futile minutes searching for other signs, Fargo quit looking. He didn't want to leave Venus hanging in the rain, but as quickly as it had started falling, it stopped. Fargo went back to the camp and got Wiley to help him cut Venus down.

They took her back to town. Water stood in the muddy streets, and the smell of rain was still in the air, but the clouds had moved on.

They located the undertaker's establishment. The sign out front said that Red Greer repaired wagons and wagon wheels and built fine cabinets and caskets.

Greer was a short man with sandy red hair and freckles spread across his face. He had broad hands and stubby fingers. When he saw who they had and had been told what had happened to her, he said, "That's Jack Lattner's work if I ever saw it."

Fargo said he wasn't so sure of that, but Greer was adamant.

"Lattner'd rather hang somebody than eat a good dinner, and he had this woman in jail to hang today. I guess he figured if he couldn't use the gallows, he'd just use a tree. He's bound to be on a tear now that somebody's burned down his jail, not to mention killed Poke Davis and shot up his other deputy."

Fargo didn't bother mentioning that he was responsible for all of the above. "Anybody seen Lattner around today?" he asked.

"Don't know about that," Greer told him. "I try to keep as far away from any news of him as I can. I'm afraid he might take a notion to hang me. He don't need a reason. Just a notion is all it takes with him. If he ain't around, all the better for the rest of us, is what I say."

"You don't reckon his wife killed him, do you?" Wiley said. "She's got a wild streak in her, and she might've taken a notion that she was tired of his way of doin' things."

"Those two grew on the same vine," Greer said. "She'd never kill him. They're too much alike." He looked over to where Venus lay. "You fellas gonna let Honoria's other girls know about her?"

Fargo said they would, and they left to go do it.

Pearl was at the Trail's End drumming up business, but Silver cried when she heard the news.

"I can't believe that even Marshal Lattner would do a thing like that," she said, wiping her eyes and reaching for the whiskey bottle. She poured a drink, took a swallow, and said, "That's a low thing to do, even for him."

"I'm not sure it was him," Fargo said. "Nobody seems to know where he is. I thought the first place he'd come would be right here."

"Well, he's not here. I don't think he'll bother us again. He's killed Venus, and that's what he wanted."

Fargo and Wiley left Silver to her whiskey. Fargo could understand why everyone thought that Lattner had been the one to kill Venus. After all, nobody had seen the man in the buffalo robe at the jail except Fargo.

"You want to go look for Pearl?" Wiley asked.

"Might as well," Fargo said, and they headed for the Trail's End.

Before they got to the saloon, they heard gunfire, and they broke into a run. But by the time they reached the batwing doors, Lattner had already killed Pearl.

Fargo pushed inside, his pistol drawn. Pearl lay on the floor by one of the tables, a pool of blood under her head. Everyone else was cowering under tables or behind the bar, which seemed to be their usual positions when there was any gun play.

Lattner fired a shot at Fargo, who jumped back outside, almost knocking Wiley over.

"Watch where you're goin'," Wiley said. "It's bad enough to have that bastard shootin' at me without you trying to flatten me at the same time."

"I am the avenging red right hand of the Lord," Lattner shouted. "I will cleanse this town of whores and robbers and sinners of every stripe."

"He's crazier than a bedbug," Wiley said. "Anytime you get a man telling you that he's doing the Lord's will by killin' somebody, you got big trouble."

"You don't have to tell me that," Fargo said.

"Either he's crazy, or he's been drinkin' too much," Wiley went on. "Whichever it is, it's bad medicine."

"I know you're out there," Lattner yelled, firing through the batwings. The bullet splintered the wood and whined away. "You're the spawn of Satan, Fargo, and I have been sent from the Lord to wipe you and your kind off the face of the earth."

"You gonna let him talk to you like that?" Wiley asked. "Go on in there and get him."

"You talk mighty big for a man who doesn't carry a gun," Fargo said.

"You could be right," Wiley admitted. "But since you're the one with the gun, you're the one who has to do something."

Fargo nodded and walked along the wall to the window that fronted the saloon. Through the wavery glass he could make out the figure of Lattner, staring at the door.

Fargo fired twice. Shattered glass flew inward. Lattner spun around and shot back, but Fargo had jumped out of sight.

"You get him?" Wiley wanted to know.

"Hit him," Fargo said. "Didn't kill him."

"Too bad. You could've finished this mess here and now."

Fargo wasn't so sure that killing Lattner would finish things. Some of the things Wiley had said earlier were worrying him in a back corner of his mind, but he didn't have time to puzzle them out right then. He returned to the window to have a look.

Lattner was gone.

Fargo went back to the door and went inside, with Wiley close behind him.

"Where's the marshal?" Fargo asked the room in general.

"Went out the back," one of the gamblers called as he crawled out from under a table.

Fargo left Wiley to see to Pearl and went out the back way. The alley was empty except for a dog that slunk away when he saw Fargo. The Trailsman could see the prints of Lattner's boots in the mud, heading in the direction of Honoria's. Fargo went that way.

After half a block, the tracks turned off between two buildings and led back to the street. Fargo followed them. When he reached the street, Fargo could see Lattner on the boardwalk. People moved aside as he came near them, even stepping into the muddy street to avoid him.

He was quite a sight, waving his pistol around and shouting at the top of his lungs as he moved along. Fargo couldn't quite make out what he was saying, but he figured it had something to do with being the Lord's appointed avenger. He also had a pretty good idea that Lattner was going to kill Silver if he got to her before Fargo could stop him, but there were too many people who had stepped back on the boardwalk after Lattner passed for Fargo to risk a shot.

"Lattner!" Fargo yelled, hoping the marshal would be distracted.

Lattner turned around and gave Fargo a casual glance. He wasn't worried about killing people, and he fired a shot at the Trailsman. The bullet plucked at Fargo's sleeve. A woman screamed and ran into Fargo's line of fire.

Reaching Honoria's tent, Lattner ducked inside. Fargo thought he heard a scream and then a gunshot. He tried to run faster, but no one moved out of his way. They weren't as afraid of him as they were of Lattner.

When he got to the tent, Fargo went in with his gun ready, but Lattner wasn't there.

Silver was. She was slumped by the table where she had been sitting with her whiskey glass. Blood stained the entire right side of her dress. Lattner had been in too much of a hurry to take his time with her, and he had already fled out the back of the tent.

"Somebody really needs to kill that son of a bitch," Silver said, her voice pinched with pain. "And somebody tried. He's wounded, but he's strong as a bull."

Fargo helped her into a chair.

"Don't worry about me," she said. "I'll be all right. I think it might have broken a rib, but that won't kill me. Go after that crazy marshal before he guns down everybody in town."

"You're bleeding," Fargo said. "I can fix you up."

"It's just a crease. I'll get over it. Help me pour some whiskey and go after Lattner. I can get myself to a doctor."

Fargo picked up a glass and set it on the table. Then he poured it full of spirit.

"That'll do just fine," Silver said, taking hold of the glass, and Fargo left her there.

He thought there were only a couple of places that Lattner might be going, and one of them was his house. Sure enough, that's the way the prints in the mud led. Things were coming together for Fargo now. He still hadn't quite figured out all of it, but a lot of little things were making sense.

Fargo went back to the saloon, but Wiley wasn't there. The man who'd taken over as bartender told Fargo that Wiley had gone with several other men to take Pearl to Greer's undertaking business.

"Is there a shotgun under that bar?" Fargo asked.

"I never looked," the man said.

"Well, look now," Fargo told him.

The man bent over and looked. When he stood up again, he was holding an old shotgun.

"Sure enough," he said. "There was one."

Fargo had figured there might be. In a place like Devil's Creek, it paid to keep a gun handy. Too bad for the former bartender that he hadn't had the time or the sense to use it.

"I need to borrow it," Fargo said.

"You're welcome to it. It ain't mine." As the bartender shrugged, he handed the shotgun over. Fargo checked to see if it was loaded—it was. Fargo thanked the bartender and left.

Wiley was standing just outside the open doors of Greer's talking to a couple of men when Fargo got there. When he saw Fargo, he broke away from the group and joined his friend.

"Maybe I should've been an undertaker," Wiley said. "That's one business that never runs out of customers, 'specially in a place like Devil's Creek. And I hope the next customer is Jack Lattner. Did you get him yet?"

"Not yet," Fargo said, and he handed the shotgun to Wiley. "I think I managed to hurry him a little when he tried to kill Silver, though, so Greer won't be having to fit a casket to her this time."

"That's good," Wiley said. He took the shotgun gingerly, as if Fargo had handed him a diamondback rattler. He looked it over and said, "What's this for?"

"I've decided it's time you started helping out a little more," Fargo said. "If you'd had this back at the Trail's End a while ago, we wouldn't still be chasing after Lattner."

"We're gonna chase him?"

"That's right. Come on."

"Where we headed?"

"Lattner's house. I'm pretty sure that's where he's holed up."

"How do you know he's not tryin' to kill somebody else? He's on a real rampage."

"He'll probably go on another sooner or later, but not right now."

"You sound mighty sure of that."

"I think he's hurt. I'm not certain how bad, but let's stop wasting time."

Fargo turned and walked away, trusting that Wiley would come along with him.

He was right. He heard Wiley squishing through the mud, and after they'd gone only a little way the old gambler caught up with him and said, "You seem sorta preoccupied, Fargo. You got all this figgered out by now?"

"I've told you that I'm not sure about anything," Fargo said. "I could be dead wrong."

They walked a few more paces before Wiley said, "Well, are you gonna tell me about it, or not, dammit?"

"I'll tell you," Fargo said, "seeing that you're the one who helped me figure it out."

"I did?" Wiley didn't seem convinced. "How'd I manage to do that?"

"If a man keeps talking long enough, sooner or later he might say something that makes sense."

"I guess you mean that as a compliment," Wiley said, rubbing his beard. "Maybe I'm smarter than you thought."

"I don't think *smart* has anything to do with it. Even a blind hog comes up with an acorn now and then."

"Well, hell, long as I come up with the answer, what does it matter if I'm a blind hog? Now, you gonna tell me about it or not?"

"I'll tell you if you'll shut up for a minute," Fargo said.

"You won't hear another word out of me till the story's told. Go ahead and get to it."

So Fargo told him.

17

"There were a couple of things," Fargo said. "When Lattner was doing the shooting, you said he was bad medicine."

"And by God he was," Wiley said. "He's bad medicine any time, but when he's got a gun or a hang rope, he's worse than that. I don't see how that could be any help to you."

"It was something you said earlier, something about if I thought Lattner was a medicine man."

"I don't remember that. And I don't see what difference it makes, either. Lattner wouldn't know a medicine bag from a bull's ball sac."

"This doesn't have anything to do with medicine bags," Fargo said, stepping over a puddle that reflected the blue sky. "It has to do with cactus."

Wiley said he didn't have any idea what Fargo was talking about.

"I've heard that some of the Indians in Texas use cactus buds to give themselves visions. Lattner claims to be from down that way, and that's probably where he met Maria. She might be a half-breed, but she could've learned some of the tribe's tricks if she lived with them for long enough and kept her eyes and ears open."

"Maybe," Wiley said, "but that don't mean much. She ain't the one havin' the visions."

"No, but her husband is. What if she found out that she could give him those visions and make him believe they were real? She could even prove that he was God's chosen. Look what he thinks he was able to do with Poke Davis."

"You sayin' he didn't do that?"

"I think it was Maria's doing. She gave him a little bit of self-respect, and Lattner did the rest."

"How'd she go about doin' that?" Wiley asked. "By givin' him some of that cactus juice?"

"I don't know how she did it," Fargo said. "I can guess, though."

"Well, go ahead and guess. I don't see nobody stoppin' you."

"Maria's the kind of woman who likes to take control of men. Like she did Billy. I think she did the same thing with Davis."

Wiley thought that one over. Then he said, "He was kind of short for that, wasn't he?"

"I hope you don't think *tall* means *long*," Fargo said. "Do you?"

"Come to think of it, I guess not. I knew a short fella once that was hung like a damn mule. But then he wasn't near as short as Poke was. Besides, that don't explain why things went to hell in this town."

"Yes, it does. Maria was behind everything. Samuel practically told me that. She's always wanted what she gave Poke."

"Some nooky?" Wiley asked.

"No, some respect. And with everyone in town scared to death of Lattner, she has it. She can do whatever she pleases, and nobody's going to call her on it. If they do, they'll wind up dead."

"Like Honoria did. I reckon you think Maria poisoned her."

"Now you're catching on. She was in the tent right before Honoria died. Poisoning her would have been easy."

"Well, I guess I can follow all that, but that still don't tell us why Lattner wanted to hang Venus, or why he shot those other gals."

"Because Maria told him to. I think she had him believing that surviving that hanging down in Texas and the change in Poke, along with his visions, meant he's exactly what he keeps telling us he is: the Lord's avenger."

"Why's he after you, though?"

"She doesn't like people she can't control, so she's the one who decided to get revenge."

"On you, you mean. That's who you're talkin' about."

"That's right, on me. And when Silver and Pearl took up the cause, they had to die, too."

"But Lattner wasn't after you until just now. He never took a shot at you before there in the Trail's End."

"That's because Maria wasn't sure about me earlier. Now she is."

"That just about explains it, I guess, except for where Lattner's been all this time."

"In his house. Maria must've given him an extra strong dose. From what I've heard, those cactus buds can put you to sleep for a good while. Fact of the matter, Lattner was already looking pretty sleepy when I saw him the other day. Sleepy and crazy. Anyway, they must've been in the house when we came by looking for him yesterday. I thought so, but I wasn't sure. I should have just broken down the door."

They were nearly at Lattner's place by that time. Wiley said, "You gonna break it down today?"

"If I have to," Fargo told him. "Could be they'll just let us in this time."

"And why in the hell would they do a thing like that?"

"Because they know I'll come right through the door anyhow."

"Yeah," Wiley said, "I guess they got that figgered out by now. Course they could be settin' up an ambush in there for us."

"I think we're about to find out," Fargo said. "You get ready with that shotgun."

"I been ready ever since we left Greer's. You tell me who you want shot, and I'll pop 'em for you."

"You sound pretty much at home with it."

"You think because I don't carry one, I don't know how to use one? I thought you knew me better than that. I could shoot out a gnat's eye at thirty paces."

"That's a shotgun you're holding," Fargo said. "Not a rifle."

"I know that. You think I don't know that? I was just giving you an example of how good a shot I am."

"Just as long as you don't think that's a rifle you're carrying."

"I know what I'm carrying," Wiley told him. "Let's get on with it."

Fargo went to the front door. Nobody offered to let him in, so he kicked it open. It slammed back against the wall with a crack like a rifle shot. Two panes of glass fell out of the frame and splintered on the floor. Just inside the entrance there were small drops of blood on the hardwood.

There didn't seem to be anyone in the house, but there was the smell of something spicy in the air, as if someone had been cooking. Or making a witch's brew.

Fargo looked in the kitchen first, with Wiley at his elbow. No one was there, but there were coals in the stove and a round black pot sat on top of it. The smell was coming from the pot. Fargo had a feeling whatever was cooking there, it wasn't supper.

"You know what?" Wiley said. "With Lattner still on his feet, you got to admit that you have a bad habit of shootin' people who just get up and go about their business when you're through with 'em."

Fargo had been so busy puzzling out the cause of Lattner's madness that he hadn't thought about the ghost. He'd put his mind to it later if need be. Right now, they had to find Lattner.

"Lattner won't be on his feet long," Fargo said. "He's hurt."

"Yeah, but he's still dangerous, hurt or not. Where you reckon he is?"

"He must be in the bedroom," Fargo said. "You stick close to me. I don't want you pulling the trigger on that thing while I'm in front of you."

"I'm beginnin' to get the idea that you don't trust me with this gun," Wiley said.

"I trust you. I just want to get out of this with a whole skin."

"I ain't gonna shoot you, so don't you worry about it."

Fargo worried about it nevertheless. Maybe it hadn't been such a good idea to give Wiley the shotgun.

The bedroom door was closed. Fargo kicked it open, and it swung back hard against the wall. Lattner was inside the room, lying on the bed. He was very still. Blood stained a poultice spanning his otherwise bare chest.

"Looks like you might've killed him after all," Wiley said.

He must not have noticed the pistol in Lattner's right hand, but Fargo did. He said, "Watch it," and just as the words left his mouth, Latter rose straight up into a sitting position and fired a shot that took an eighth of an inch off Wiley's left earlobe.

Wiley yelped and then said, "I'll be goddamned!" as he and Fargo ducked back to stand on either side of the doorway. Wiley held the shotgun in the crook of his arm and fumbled around for his bandana. He got it to his ear, but blood had already soaked into much of his shirt.

"Shit," Wiley said. "Good thing he's dead, or he might've killed me. Bad enough he shot my ear off. There ain't nothing that bleeds like an ear. Stings, too."

"He didn't shoot your whole ear off," Fargo told him. "Just a little piece of it."

"Still stings like the devil, though," Wiley said.

A noise came from the bedroom, and Fargo looked to see what was going on. Lattner had raised the window and was pushing himself through the opening.

Fargo hated to shoot a man in the back, but he figured he could make an exception in Lattner's case. He never found out whether he could do it because Wiley bumped his elbow with the shotgun, throwing off any chance he had of hitting the marshal.

"Didn't mean to jostle you," Wiley said. "I was just tryin' to stop my ear from bleedin', and the damn gun moved on me. Where'd he go?"

"Out the window."

"We goin' after him?"

"What do you think?"

They didn't bother with the window. They went out the front door and saw Lattner stumbling along the street.

He was obviously weak from his wound, and he didn't bother stepping over the puddles. He splashed through them without taking notice. Once he almost fell, but he righted himself and kept going. The poultice fell from his chest into the mud, but Lattner didn't notice, or if he did, he didn't care. There was a bloody poultice on his back as well, but it remained stuck in place.

"Where's he headed?" Wiley asked. He was still holding his bandana against his ear with one hand, and the shoulder of his shirt was covered with blood.

"I think he might be going to the jail."

"He's in for a little surprise, then. The jail ain't there no more."

"He might not know that. We didn't see him there last night. Besides, he's confused, and he's hurt."

"He's not the only one."

"Hasn't that ear stopped bleeding yet?"

Wiley took away the bandana. "Yeah, it seems to've stopped. But it still hurts."

"You'll get over it."

"Sure, you can say that. You ain't the one missin' half your ear."

"It's just a scratch," Fargo said. "You'll be just fine."

Wiley didn't say anything else until they had followed Lattner for a bit farther. Then he said, "Looks like he's on the way to the jail, all right. You reckon he's gonna kill anybody before we catch up with him?"

Fargo said he didn't think so. Lattner didn't seem interested in killing anyone. He was just trying to get to a place where he felt safe, like an animal returning to its den.

"Where you think his wife is?" Wiley asked. "She's bound to be the one that cooked up that poultice for him."

"We'll worry about her later," Fargo said.

The sight of Lattner's bare, bleeding chest guaranteed that nobody got in his way, and this time they didn't get in Fargo's way, either. They were too stunned by the sight of the wavering and incoherent marshal to continue on their business after they'd stepped out of his path.

When he came within sight of the burned jail, Latter swayed to a stop. Some of the gallows timbers remained upright, and one wall of the jail was still standing. Everything smelled of charred wood and rain-dampened ashes.

Like a wounded bear, Lattner stood in front of the remains of the gallows and raised his head to sniff the air. He shook his fist at the sky and howled incomprehensible words.

Quite a crowd was gathering to watch the spectacle. Most of them had probably been there the night before, Fargo thought, though he didn't recognize any of them. Lattner paid them no attention. It was as if he were oblivious to their presence. All he could see was the ruins in front of him.

"Marshal!" a voice called out from behind Fargo.

He turned to see who it was. Delong was pushing his way forward. His left arm was in a sling, and he looked a little wobbly, though not nearly as wobbly as Lattner.

"I tried to stop 'em, Marshal," Delong said, shoving through the crowd. "They wouldn't listen to me. It was Fargo's doing. All Fargo's doing."

Lattner had paid no attention to Delong at first, but when he heard Fargo's name, he turned. His chest was raw and red where the bullet had gone in. Fargo figured the wound on his back looked even worse.

Lattner looked at Fargo and smiled. The hang-rope scar around his neck pulsed as if it were alive. He raised his pistol.

"Marshal," Delong said, and Lattner shot him. The bullet went in Delong's right eye and came out the back of his head, taking half his skull off with it. Delong jerked back two steps and fell. Lattner turned around and looked at the jail and gallows as if nothing had happened.

Wiley looked down at the deputy and said, "Not much doubt about Lattner killin' what he shoots at. Unless maybe he was shootin' at you."

"I think he was," Fargo said. "No reason for him to kill Delong."

"Well, what're we gonna do about it?"

"We can't just shoot him."

"Maybe you can't," Wiley said. "But I sure as hell can."

He raised the shotgun, but Fargo said, "Don't. There are a lot of things we still don't know."

Wiley didn't lower the shotgun. He held it steady and asked, "Like what?"

"Like whether he was the one who locked me in that cell last night."

"I thought about that. Had to be him. He's the one had the keys. Delong told us that. Remember?"

"He could have given the keys to someone."

"Who?"

"His wife."

"Looks like you'd have known if it was her."

"Whoever it was had on that buffalo robe. And wasn't as big as Lattner, either. Maria's a big woman. It could've been her."

x

135

18

"Jail's kind of a mess," Fargo said.

Lattner didn't appear to hear him. He stood there slack-jawed, staring straight ahead.

"It was your wife who got you into all this," Fargo said. "You aren't the avenging arm of the Lord, Lattner. You aren't even a very good marshal."

Lattner's gun hand twitched, but only a little. There was no other sign that he'd heard.

"I want to know something," Fargo said. "Was it you who came in the jail after me last night and locked me in a cell?"

Lattner's head turned slowly, and he looked at Fargo with eyes so dull that Fargo knew the life was leaving them.

"I didn't know about . . . this," he said, turning back to the jail and gesturing with his empty hand. His voice was expressionless. "I didn't know."

Fargo believed him, which meant that it hadn't been Lattner in the burning jail last night. He said, "You look tired, Lattner. Give me that pistol, and I'll help you find a doctor. You need someone to dress that wound."

Up close, the wound looked even worse, and there was a smell about it. It seemed to be festering already.

"Maria fixed me up," Lattner said. The same flat voice. "Maria always fixes me up."

Fargo didn't think there was anything she could do for him this time. Or maybe she'd already done it. Maybe the poultice had been made to guarantee Lattner's death rather than his life. Fargo found himself almost feeling sorry for the dying marshal, who probably didn't even realize the havoc he'd wrought in Devil's Creek.

"Why did you hang Billy Banks?" Fargo asked him.

"Did I do that?"

"You did it, all right. Did Maria tell you to?"

"Is he the one who consorted with whores?" Lattner asked.

His eyes had a faraway look now, as if he were staring at some distant horizon no one else could see. He probably was, and it was the horizon of a country Fargo didn't want to travel to anytime soon.

"That might have been me," Fargo said. "Not Billy."

Lattner's eyes turned to Fargo again, and just for a second they cleared. He said, "Yes, that was you. But the other one, too. He had to meet the Lord's justice."

Maria was the crazy one, Fargo now realized, not Lattner. He had just been another of her victims. He reached for Lattner's elbow to help him move away from the ruins of the jail.

"You have to meet the Lord's justice, too," Lattner said, and his pistol swung up.

But he was dying now, slow and weak, and Fargo grabbed his wrist and twisted the gun away from him before he could fire.

Lattner stared down at his empty hand.

"What's happening to me?" he said. "What's—"

Fargo stepped away from him, and the big man fell face forward into the mud of the street, making a wet splash when he hit. His right foot jerked twice and then was still.

"You reckon he's really dead this time?" Wiley asked, coming to stand beside Fargo, who stood looking down at the body.

"He's been dead for the last minute or two," Fargo said. "He just didn't know it yet."

The people in the crowd drew closer, all of them careful to step around Delong as they made their way forward. Everyone wanted to have a look at the marshal now that he was no longer a threat to anyone. A boy about ten years old bent over and poked Lattner's shoulder. A woman in a bonnet dragged him away from the body. He dug his heels into the mud, but she managed to move him back into the crowd.

"Hell of a thing," Wiley said. "Lattner dyin' like that and not tellin' you what you wanted to know."

"He told me about Billy."

"I heard that part. Billy didn't really associate with those whores. He had a drink with one of 'em a time or two at the Trail's End, that's all."

"Maria wouldn't have liked that, and you know Billy would have called her on it if she said anything."

"Yeah, you're right about that. You want to go tell Greer he's got himself another couple of customers?"

"He's going to want to know who's paying for all this," Fargo said.

"You don't have to worry about Greer," Wiley said with a crooked grin. "The undertaker is one man who always gets paid." He nudged Lattner with a toe. "He's dead, all right. So where does that leave us, Fargo? All squared away?"

"Not as long as Maria's on the loose."

"You want me to hang on to this shotgun, then?"

"I think that might be a good idea," Fargo said.

Greer had a little wagon that they drove to the jail. Most of the crowd had returned to their business by the time he got there. Now that Lattner was dead, they seemed to have lost interest in him. A couple of men had stayed around, and they helped Wiley and Fargo load the marshal and his deputy into the wagon. It was barely wide enough for the two of them to lie side by side. They were covered in mud and blood.

"Those fellas are a hell of a mess," Greer said. "I guess I can clean 'em up a little. Not much I can do about Delong, though. His own mama wouldn't know him. Seems like kind of a waste, anyhow, them being dead and all. They won't know the difference."

"I'll know," Fargo told him, and something in his tone caused Greer to look up.

"Sure, sure, I know just what you mean. I'll take care of everything. Clean 'em up as best I can. You don't have to worry about me. You fellas going to be at the funeral?"

"Don't count on us," Fargo said.

Greer nodded. "Knowing the way folks felt about these two, I won't count on anybody to show up except the preacher."

"Don't count on him, either," Fargo said.

Fargo went by the Cottons' store first, but Ruth wasn't there. Fargo had been afraid that would be the case. It would have been too much to hope for.

Bob Cotton, a young man with a craggy face and strong hands, said that she was out. "What is it that you want with her?"

He seemed suspicious, not that Fargo could blame him.

"I'm the one who guided her here," Fargo said. "I just wanted to let her know I was leaving."

Cotton apparently couldn't see anything wrong with that. He said, "She's over at the church. She does love that brother of hers, and it's easy to see why. He's a fine man, dedicated to stamping out sin here in our little town."

"So was the marshal," Fargo said. "It didn't work out so well for him."

"Samuel's not like that. Have you met him?"

Fargo said that he had.

"Then you know what he's like. If you're riding out that way, tell him I said good morning."

Fargo had his own thoughts about Samuel, but he wasn't going to let Cotton in on them.

"I'll give him your regards," Fargo said.

"I think Bob Cotton's a fine young fella," Wiley said as they rode along. "He'll make that Ruth a good husband. Not a harder worker in the town."

"I'm just hoping Ruth will still be around when we get to the church," Fargo said.

"Sure she'll be around. What're you worried about?"

Fargo put his heels to the big Ovaro's sides.

"Maria," he said.

The clouds were massing in back of the Bitterroots again, and Fargo was sure there was going to be another rainstorm. The wind had begun to blow, and there was a little touch of the mountain cold in the air. Wiley said it was coming down from the snow on the mountain peaks.

"This valley is pretty warm this time of year," he said, "but up there on the mountains, it's still wintertime. The snow'll melt sooner or later, but till then it can get pretty raw up there on the top."

Fargo asked if Wiley spent much time there.

"Not if I can help it. I'm too old, and my blood's thinned out. I like a nice warm saloon and some gamblers who don't mind playing cards with an old coot they think they can beat."

By the time they got to the church, the clouds had moved in, but there was no rain.

"Won't be a storm, this time," Wiley said, contradicting Fargo's earlier thought. "This'll be one of those rains that just settles in quietlike and stays for a while."

The church was quiet, dark under the clouds and in the shade of the pines that surrounded it. The wind had blown green pine needles onto the roof and all around the ground.

Fargo remembered that not too long ago he had heard Ruth and Samuel singing inside the church building. He didn't think they'd be doing much more singing together.

"Don't look like there's anybody around," Wiley said. "Reckon where they could've gone?"

Fargo said he didn't know. He'd thought he'd find all three of them there: Ruth, Samuel, and Maria.

"They might be inside," he said. "We'll have a look."

"You thinkin' I should take the shotgun?"

"That's right. And stay with me, not behind me."

"You don't ever give a fella a chance, do you?" Wiley said. "I ain't shot you yet, have I?"

They got off their horses and went to the door of the church. It was closed but not locked. Fargo pushed it open, and as it swung out of the way, he and Wiley went inside the little building.

The church was dark and full of shadows. The only sounds were the ones made by the wind as it blew through the eaves and the chinks in the log walls.

"Told you there wasn't anybody here," Wiley said after a second or two. "Let's get out of here. It's downright spooky, and I don't feel right, somehow or another, havin' a gun in church."

"Hold on," Fargo said. "Don't be in such a rush. There's somebody here, all right."

"Where is he, then?"

Fargo pointed. "Look up there by the altar."

The rough-hewn altar stood at the end of the narrow aisle. It looked as though Samuel or some member of the

141

congregation had carved it from the trunk of a pine, and it leaned just a little to the left. Beside it sat a dark, motionless figure that seemed almost like another carved object.

"You right sure that's somebody?" Wiley asked.

Fargo was sure. He said, "Let's go have a look-see."

As they started down the center aisle between the wooden pews, the figure rose slowly from the floor, and they could see that it was clothed in a buffalo robe.

"Shit!" Wiley said. "It's Tom!" He paused and glanced up at the church roof. "I didn't mean that 'shit' part, Lord. It just sorta slipped out."

The figure stood there looking at them, its face hidden in the shadow of the hat pulled down low over its forehead.

"That's not Tom," Fargo said. "Take another look."

Wiley stopped and stared. Nothing he saw appeared to change his opinion.

"It sure as hell looks like the way you said Tom did. And if I was a ghost, I think I'd go lookin' for a church to hide myself in. Better there than the graveyard."

"It's not a ghost, either."

"You seem to know a hell of a lot about who it is all of a sudden," Wiley said. He looked at the roof again. "Beggin' your pardon, Lord, about that 'hell.' You know I didn't really mean it."

"I don't think the Lord minds a little cussing," Fargo said. "If he does, it's too late for you already."

"I wish you wouldn't say things like that. And I'm gonna cuss again if you don't do something about that ghost."

"I told you that it's not a ghost. It's Samuel."

"The preacher? Why in the hell would he be dressed up like Tom?"

"Tell him why, Samuel," Fargo said. "I'd sort of like to know the answer to that one myself."

"I believe you already know more than you want me to think you do, Fargo," Samuel said in a loud voice that echoed from the walls of the church. It was the voice he must have used to deliver his sermons. "Why don't you tell him?"

"I wish somebody'd tell me," Wiley said. "I thought you were a ghost, or maybe a man who'd got shot and wanted to make up for it, and now I find out you're just a preacher dressed up like one or the other. Don't make a bit of sense to me no matter how I look at it."

"It makes sense if you think about it for a while," Fargo said. "I should've figured it all out a long time ago, back when Lattner knew my name the first time he saw me."

"You thought Maria told him."

"She said it wasn't her, and I believed her. I was right. The one who told him was Samuel. He's the only other one who could have done it, and he's the one who halfway believed that Lattner was sent to Devil's Creek by God. He's the one who hates whores as much as Lattner did. He and Lattner have been working together all along. Or he and Maria. Or all three of them."

Wiley was still puzzled. "What difference does that make? Even if it's right, Samuel oughtn't to have anything against you. He never saw you before the other day."

"That's right, Samuel," Fargo said. "So tell us what you have against me."

Samuel raised his left arm to point at Fargo. His right hand remained inside the buffalo robe.

"You made Ruth into a whore. She was married to a fine man with a fine name, and you changed her to one of the daughters of Sodom."

"A name like Moses doesn't make you a fine man," Fargo said. "And you didn't know anything about me and Ruth the first time you tried to kill me."

"I could tell what you had done, a man and a woman on the trail alone. The smell of her sin was on her. I had a buffalo robe, so I dressed as one of the men you killed. I hoped you'd think he had come for you."

"I did for a while, but I usually kill whoever I shoot."

"Didn't kill Lattner," Wiley said.

"He's dead," Fargo said. "Just took him some time. But then Samuel already knows about Lattner. Isn't that right, Samuel?"

"That's right. I have received the word."

"You make that sound pretty fancy," Fargo said. "Why didn't you just say Maria told you?"

"What's Maria got to do with it, anyhow?" Wiley said. "I'm still a little behind on all this."

"It's always been Maria," Fargo told him. "I wondered why Samuel didn't seem to want his own sister around him.

The first thing he did was find somebody for her to stay with. Well, he didn't want her around because he and Maria were humping like minks every chance they got."

"That's a lie!" Samuel's voice boomed out and seemed to rattle the walls. "We never committed that sin!"

"I don't care what you call it," Fargo said, "but you were doing it. Maria couldn't get close to a man with out getting him into bed, and she's bound to have gotten you there, too. Must have made you feel really good, thinking that you were betraying Lattner, just maybe a man chosen by God. You were on his side, even helping him when you could, and at the same time you were flouncing in bed with his wife every chance you got. Or maybe you didn't feel guilty at all. You don't like whores, and that's all Maria is when you get right down to it."

"Liar!" Samuel screamed. "You will burn in hell for that lie, Fargo, the way you should have burned in the jail."

"You did your best," Fargo said. "You didn't let anybody see you, and they wouldn't have known you if they had."

"Satan must have helped you escape," Samuel said. "There was no other way."

Fargo gave him a thin smile. "Yes, there was. You got a set of keys from Maria or Lattner, but I had the other one. You'll have to do better than that to kill me, Samuel."

"Then I will," the preacher said, throwing back the buffalo robe and raising the Colt that he held in his right hand.

Fargo had been waiting for something like that. Samuel was no gunman, and he didn't have a chance. Fargo drew and shot him twice before the preacher could pull the trigger. Samuel dropped the pistol and slumped over against the altar in an attempt to keep himself from falling, but he didn't have enough strength left to hold himself up. He slid slowly to the floor and lay still.

"I don't like this even a little bit," Wiley said. "Killin' a preacher's one thing, and that's bad enough. But killin' one inside his own church ain't likely to get you on God's good side."

"I don't think God's going to miss Samuel a whole lot," Fargo said. "He wasn't exactly doing the Lord's work."

"Some of the time he was. You gotta give him credit for that."

Fargo didn't feel like giving Samuel credit for anything. He walked up to the altar and knelt down beside the preacher.

"You still there, Samuel?" he said.

"Still . . . here," Samuel answered in a muffled voice nothing at all like the one that had boomed out earlier.

"Then you need to tell me one thing before the devil comes to claim you," Fargo said. "Where's Ruth?"

"She . . . has to be punished. For what you did to her."

"You son of a bitch. Tell me where she is. Now."

"Maria will punish her. Maria will . . ."

Samuel's voice trailed away, and he lay still.

"A man ought not to say 'son of a bitch' in church," Wiley said. " 'Specially not a preacher."

"I didn't think something like that would bother a man with a mouth like yours," Fargo told him.

"You got a point," Wiley said. "Is that son of a bitch dead yet?"

"Not yet." Fargo stood up. "But near enough. We still have us one more job to do. Let's get out of this place."

19

The sky was black and the clouds were heavy with rain. Fargo spotted the tracks of two horses just as raindrops started to drift down, slowly at first and then a little harder, the wind driving them along.

"They're headed up toward the mountains," Fargo said, pulling his slicker on.

"Damn," Wiley said. "Lots of places to get lost in up there. Cold up there, too, like I said."

"You don't have to go if you don't want to."

"You think you can get rid of me that easy? I got you into this mess 'cause I thought all you had to do was come here and kill the marshal. I didn't know it was gonna get so damn complicated and turn out not to be the marshal's fault after all. But by God I don't quit on a man when I start ridin' a trail with him just because things are a little rougher than I thought they'd be."

"I didn't think you would. But it's probably a lot warmer and drier back in that saloon at a card table."

"Don't tempt me, Fargo. I'm not a quitter, but I can be tempted. Even a preacher can be tempted. Samuel found that out."

Fargo didn't think it had taken much to tempt Samuel, who struck the Trailsman as the kind of man who was just waiting for temptation to come along so he could give in to it. When he did, he could never see the sin in himself, but he could see it all too clearly in everyone else, and that was what made him so dangerous. Fargo had known too many men like that.

He'd known too many women like Maria, too, seemingly eager for sex and life but at the same time hating anyone who opposed their own whims. She'd brought about the end of Billy Banks and who knew how many others, besides setting up men like Poke Davis and giving them the power to take life anytime they wanted to. Poke had been just as much a dupe as Lattner, and he'd known as little about the way he was being controlled as the marshal had. Devil's Creek had the right name, Fargo thought, but in this case the devil was a woman.

The rain swished down through the trees, and Fargo wondered what Ruth thought about all that had happened. She'd been betrayed by her own brother and handed over to a woman who was certainly going to kill her if Fargo and Wiley didn't stop it. She must have been disappointed and surprised at Samuel, and she must have wondered what had happened to the brother she knew.

Maria had happened, of course. She had achieved the respect she craved and was the virtual ruler of Devil's Creek, free to enjoy every man she wanted, but things had started to come apart when Fargo came on the scene.

Wiley broke into Fargo's thoughts.

"You won't be able to follow these tracks for long," he said. "Rain will wash 'em out eventually, and then where will be be?"

"We won't be in the mountains," Fargo said. "That's for sure."

"Why not? The tracks are goin' in that direction."

"The mountains are a little too far. Maria's going to want to do something before long. And I wouldn't be surprised if she'll wait for us if we don't catch up to her."

"Why would she do a crazy thing like that?"

Fargo started to say she'd do it because she was crazy, but he decided to explain things a little more clearly.

"She'd do it because she doesn't just want to kill Ruth. You heard Samuel. She wants to punish her. Maria likes to punish people."

"I don't see what you're gettin' at."

"I'm getting at the point of what Maria wants to do. Just killing Ruth wouldn't serve any purpose. Maria likes for people to die in front of an audience. That's why Lattner had hangings."

"Won't be much of an audience," Wiley said. "Just the two of us."

"I don't want to hurt your feelings," Fargo said, "but I'm the only one who matters."

"Don't hurt my feelin's a bit. You gonna tell me why, though?"

"Because I think Samuel told Maria about me and Ruth. Killing her will punish me, too."

"But we ain't gonna let that happen, are we?"

"I hope not," Fargo said. "But I can't promise you a thing. Except that you're going to get wet."

"I'm already wetter than a drownded rat. Won't hurt me to get a little more water on me."

"Might even be good for you," Fargo said.

"Now that does hurt my feelin's," Wiley said. "I bathe as reg'lar as any man in Devil's Creek."

"Which is none too regular."

Wiley didn't have an answer for that, and they rode along wordlessly in the wind and the drifting rain.

They lost the tracks only a few minutes later, but they kept riding in the same direction. Fargo was sure that Maria would be waiting for them as soon as she found a place she liked. He even had an idea what kind of place it would be. And then he had another thought: What if Maria decided to kill Ruth without an audience, the way Venus had been killed? Fargo was fairly sure that Maria had taken a hand in that particular hanging, simply because she would have wanted to do so. She hadn't shown herself to Fargo then. That wasn't necessary, as long as Venus had died and Fargo knew it. All of which meant that Ruth might already be dead, killed before Fargo could do a thing to help her.

He told himself it hadn't happened that way, and not just because he didn't want Ruth to die. That was part of it, but the other part was that Fargo felt an obligation to her. In a sense he'd gotten her into this situation. She'd played her own part, but it wasn't her fault that her brother was involved with Lattner and Maria.

It wasn't Fargo's fault, either, but if he'd only realized earlier what was going on, he could have prevented some of it. Or maybe not. It didn't matter now. The only thing that mattered was saving Ruth.

"You seem to be in a mighty big hurry all of a sudden," Wiley called out.

Fargo saw that he'd ridden far ahead of the old gambler, leaving him a dim sight back in the rain. Fargo pulled back on the Ovaro's reins and waited for Wiley to catch up with him.

"I was worried about Ruth," Fargo said when Wiley reached him.

"I don't blame you. If Maria's as bad as you say she is, Ruth's in a world of trouble. But you weren't in such a hurry a while back."

"I got worried that Maria might kill her without me being there to watch."

"Now, do you really believe that, after what you told me?"

"I'm not sure. I'd hate for it to happen that way and for me and you to show up just a few minutes late."

"A few or a lot, it won't make any difference to Ruth," Wiley said.

"It would make a big difference to me."

"Yeah, I can see that it would. So why are we goin' so slow?"

They touched up their mounts and rode on. Before they'd gone far, Wiley had a question for Fargo.

"You say Maria wants you to see her kill Ruth, ain't that right?"

"That's the way I see it."

"Well, then, I been thinkin' about that. There's something that don't quite work out right."

"What's that?"

"How does Maria figger she's gonna get away from you after Ruth is dead? Assumin' that she dies, of course, which we ain't gonna let happen. But what if it does?"

"I don't think Maria cares about getting away anymore," Fargo said. "Lattner's dead, so whatever power she had in Devil's Creek is over. Samuel's dead, so there's nothing left for her with him."

"She don't know about him, though."

"If she sees us, she'll know," Fargo said.

"Yeah, I guess she will. And she wouldn't have figgered he could stop us, not after as many tries as he's had."

"So there's not much left for her, except for the satisfaction of having me see Ruth die."

"Then she's bound to wait for us."

"I hope you're right about that," Fargo said.

Maria had chosen her spot well. It was a small clearing dominated on one side by a giant cottonwood tree with thick limbs and a mottled trunk. Ruth was sitting on a horse beneath the cottonwood. Her hands were tied behind her back, and a hanging noose was fixed around her neck. The hang rope had been tied to the trunk of the cottonwood and thrown over one of the broad branches. It was stretched almost taut, and Fargo could see that Ruth was struggling to control the horse she straddled to keep it from moving forward. Ruth hadn't put on a slicker, or hadn't been allowed to, and her clothes clung heavily to the ripe curves of her body. She was shivering with the cold, which made it all the more difficult for her to control the horse. When she saw Fargo and Wiley, she made an effort to smile, but it wasn't very successful.

There was no sign of Maria.

Wiley said, "Looks like Maria figgered out she couldn't get away from us and did a halfway job of things."

Fargo didn't think so. He said, "She doesn't work that way. She's around here somewhere. Isn't that right, Ruth?"

As if afraid to speak for fear she might spook the horse, Ruth gave a nod, the best one she could, considering the rope around her neck.

The sky was dark and rain dripped from the trees. Somewhere back in the shadows Maria was hiding, waiting and watching, but Fargo couldn't see her. He thought he knew what her plan was, however. As soon as he made a move toward Ruth, Maria would most likely fire a gun to get the horse moving under Ruth. Maybe she'd even shoot Fargo, though she wouldn't want to kill him. She'd just want to knock him out of the saddle and keep him from getting to Ruth. She'd wait and kill him after Ruth was dead.

So Fargo didn't go anywhere. He just sat on the Ovaro and watched and listened.

Wiley got impatient after only a few minutes had passed. He said, "What're we waitin' for, Fargo? Let's go get that little gal and get outta here."

"I don't think that would be a good idea," Fargo said, and told him why.

Wiley didn't believe it. "Maria would've showed herself by now if she was here. And even if she is, we might as well do somethin'. All we've got now is some kind of half-assed standoff.''

Fargo thought it over. If he rode fast enough and got low enough in the saddle, he might be able to get to Ruth before Maria shot him. On the other hand, she might just shoot the horse out from under him, and then where would he be?

"What if I'm right and you're wrong?" Wiley asked. "What if she's gettin' away right now, laughin' her head off at us because we're sitting here watchin' that gal suffer over there and not doin' a thing to help?"

That was a possiblity, but Fargo didn't believe it for a minute. He'd been hoping to wait Maria out, see what she would do, but Wiley didn't seem to have the patience for that. So Fargo thought he'd have to try something different.

"You ride to the right," he told Wiley. "I'll ride left, and we'll meet at that cottonwood tree. If Maria's out there, there's two of us and only one of her, so one of us ought to be able to get to the tree and cut that rope."

"That sounds like a good idea to me," Wiley said. " 'Bout time we did something instead of just sittin' on our butts."

He started to move out, but a voice from the trees on the opposite side of the clearing stopped him. It was Maria's. She said, "If either one of you moves, I'll start the horse."

"I'll be damned," Wiley said. "She was back in there all the time. What do we do now?"

"Same thing we were doing before," Fargo said. "We wait."

"Shit. I never was any good at that."

"You're a card player. You know how to wait."

"That's different. And a hell of a lot drier."

The rain had let up, but water still dripped from the leaves and the ends of pine needles. Fargo thought the sky was a little lighter, but he wasn't sure. He shifted in the saddle. He was good at waiting. He wondered about Maria.

After several minutes had passed, Maria said, "You should never have come to Devil's Creek, Fargo."

"Wouldn't have if your husband hadn't killed Billy Banks," Wiley said.

"That boy? He should have stayed away from whores. Where's Samuel?"

"Waiting for you," Fargo said.

Maria seemed to know what he meant. She said, "Why don't you try to save the woman, Fargo? She tied the noose with her own hands, just the way the other whore did. You didn't have a chance to save her, but you can save this one."

Fargo didn't answer, and it was quiet for a while. Then Wiley whispered, "You were always a good shot, Fargo. Can't you just shoot the rope in half?"

"Maybe. Maria would just shoot Ruth if I did that."

"Damn. Looks like we're gonna be sittin' here the rest of our lives, starin' at those trees and talkin' to somebody we can't see."

"It won't last that long," Fargo said.

"It will if we don't do something, and it don't look like we are."

"We're doing something. We're waiting."

"I got Maria's plan figgered out, then. She's gonna wait till we're drownded or die of the grippe."

"She can't wait that long. She'll do something sooner or later."

"I hope it's sooner. What'll we do when she does it?"

"That all depends on what she does."

"Shit," Wiley said, and they waited some more.

It was at least fifteen minutes before anything happened. Finally Maria said, "I thought you were more of a man, Fargo, than to let a woman die without helping her."

"She's not dying," Fargo said.

"Now she is," Maria said, and there was the sound of pistol fire.

The bullets splatted into the wet ground near the hooves of Ruth's horse, and it reared up before jumping forward and breaking into a run. Ruth spun at the end of the rope.

"Go!" Fargo said, and spurred the Ovaro into the clearing.

Wiley was right beside him. A bullet ripped the air between them.

"If she gets me," Fargo said, "you cut Ruth down."

Wiley didn't answer. Fargo felt something burn across his right shoulder, but he didn't slow down. He and Wiley reached Ruth at about the same time. Wiley caught her in his arms, and Fargo rode to the cottonwood tree to cut the rope.

Maria shot Wiley first, and then she shot at Fargo again and missed. Wiley stayed on his horse, still supporting Ruth. Fargo reached the tree and pulled a knife from his boot, slashing the rope, splitting it easily.

When the rope parted, Ruth and Wiley both fell to the wet earth. Fargo rode over and slid off the Ovaro. He cut the ropes that held Ruth's hands, and she took the noose from her neck.

Blood was pulsing from Wiley's thigh.

"Only damn place on me there's any meat," Wiley said.

Fargo cut his pants leg away and saw that the bullet hadn't really done much damage.

"Just took a little chunk of fat off you," he said. "You'll never miss it."

"I'll miss it. I like every single bit of me."

Fargo told him to be quiet and asked Ruth if she could bandage him up.

"Yes. But what about you?"

There was blood mixed with the water on Fargo's slicker, but not much. The bullet had plowed a shallow trench across the top of his shoulder. It burned, but it wouldn't kill him.

"I'll be all right. I'm going after Maria. You two can wait for an hour, but if I'm not back by then, get Wiley back to town for a doctor."

"I'm just as tough as you are," Wiley said.

"Tougher, I'd say, but you don't need to be out here after dark with a good-looking young woman. No telling what kind of trouble you'd get into."

"You're right about that. You get that Maria, you hear?"

"I'll get her," Fargo said.

20

Water continued to drip out of the trees, but the rain no longer fell. The sky, however, got no lighter because the sun had gone down behind the Bitterroots. The woods were dark and getting darker. Fargo wondered if Maria knew her way around in them, but he didn't think it was likely. She had spent most of her time in town, too occupied to go exploring. He didn't know his way around either, but he thought he'd be better at finding it than she was.

The wet ground made her trail easy to follow, and she hadn't gone too far before Fargo realized that she had made a turn and headed back in the direction of town. He made sure he was right and then rode back to the clearing to get Ruth and Wiley.

"You should've kept after her," Wiley said. "She's gonna get away."

"I think I know where she's going," Fargo said. "And even if I'm wrong, she's not going to get away. There's no place in Devil's Creek for her to hide."

"I hope you're right. Where's she goin' then, if you're so smart?"

"Samuel's church," Fargo said. "I told her he was waiting for her."

Wiley looked at Ruth. "You didn't mention how he was doin', though."

"I think she knew that. Let's go find out."

"You're the boss," Wiley said.

On the way back to the church, Wiley complained about his leg while Ruth told them what had happened.

After Lattner was shot, Maria had come to the church

154

to see Samuel. Ruth had been surprised to see her, but Samuel hadn't.

"It didn't take me long to see that there was something between them," Ruth said. "When I found out what it was, I couldn't believe it at first."

"Samuel started out good," Wiley said. "He just lost his way. A woman can do that to a man."

"But to turn over his own sister to somebody to be killed? What kind of a man does that?"

"A confused one," Fargo said. "Samuel was all mixed up in his head about Lattner, and what he and Maria were doing didn't make things any easier for him. That doesn't excuse him, though."

"No," Ruth said. "It doesn't. He even tied my hands while she held the gun on me."

"Not easy to ride, tied up like that," Wiley said.

"I nearly fell a couple of times. She didn't care. She said I'd just have to walk if I fell."

"She untie you so you could make that noose?"

"She lied about that," Ruth said. "She tied the noose. She enjoyed it."

"I bet she did," Wiley said.

It was almost completely dark when they reached the church. The clouds covered the sky, and Fargo could barely see the outline of the building as they approached.

"You reckon she's in there?" Wiley said.

Fargo saw a dark shadow move at the side of the building. It was Maria's horse.

"She's in there," he said. "She and Samuel."

Wiley had told Ruth what had happened with Samuel. She was grieved, but it was no worse than she'd been expecting to hear. She'd lost a husband and a brother in just a short time, but Fargo thought she had the gumption to get through it.

"You goin' in after her?" Wiley asked.

"Unless you want to do it," Fargo said.

"I could do it, but I had a better idea."

"What's that?"

"I thought we'd just wait."

Fargo laughed. "Sometimes that works, sometimes it doesn't. I don't think this is the time for it."

"Well, you go on ahead then. Me and Ruth'll wait for you out here."

The church sat there in front of them, black and silent. Fargo rode up to the front door and slipped off his horse. He stood to the side and pushed the door. It swung open. The inside of the building was as dark as the bottom of a silver mine Fargo had once been in, and just as dangerous. Fargo expected pistol fire at any second, but none came.

He went inside, hoping that Maria couldn't see any better than he could. He looked toward the altar, but it was too dark for him to see anything at all. He stood very still against the wall, looking out of the corners of his eyes. In the dark, that often worked better than staring.

He still saw no movement. If Maria was there, she was keeping very quiet. Fargo decided to risk having a look at the altar. He moved into the aisle, his pistol in his hand, and walked quietly between the pews.

When he got to the altar, he saw Samuel's body, looking somehow smaller. It took Fargo just a second to figure out why. Then he put out his hand to make sure the darkness wasn't fooling him.

It wasn't. Samuel was there, all right. But he was no longer wearing the buffalo robe.

"Shit," Fargo said, thinking that Maria had outsmarted him for sure, this time.

He turned and ran down the aisle, throwing open the door when he reached it. He had to warn Wiley and Ruth.

He was too late. He heard Wiley yell, "Goddamn! It's Tom!"

Fargo saw the dark shape of Maria, wearing the buffalo robe, running toward Ruth and Wiley from the side of the church. He saw the flame leap from the muzzle of her pistol as she fired at them. Fargo was about to shoot her when he heard the roar of the shotgun.

Maria stopped as if she'd run into a wall. There was another shotgun blast, and Maria backed up two quick steps. She swayed there for a second and then fell. She didn't move again.

Fargo walked over to her and bent over to make sure she was dead. She was, and he stood up.

"Did I kill the son of a bitch?" Wiley called out.

"You did," Fargo said.

"What about Maria?"

"You killed her," Fargo said.

"I did? I thought I killed Tom."

Fargo walked over and explained what had happened.

"Well, it nearly worked," Wiley said. "I thought for sure that damned Tom had come back again, either him or Samuel's ghost. Good thing I know how to use a shotgun."

Fargo agreed that it was a good thing.

"I told you I knew all about it. You just never believe me."

"I never doubted you for a minute," Fargo said.

"Seemed to me that you did. You got anybody else to kill, or do you think this will finish it?"

"This will finish it," Fargo said.

"Good," Wiley said. "Because my leg hurts, and I think I could use a good stiff drink. You gonna get me to a doctor, or you gonna see if there's one that can help Maria?"

"Nobody can help Maria," Fargo said.

The sun was shining the next day when Fargo got ready to leave Devil's Creek. Wiley tried to talk him into staying another day.

"You oughta go to the funerals," he said. "Greer's never had to make this many caskets at one time in his life."

"I can skip the funerals," Fargo said. "I hope you're satisfied about Billy now."

"I know he's restin' in peace. I appreciate your comin' here and helpin' me out."

Fargo said Wiley was welcome.

"I guess you did a little more than help out," Wiley said.

"A man can't stand by when there's something rotten going on. Not when his friend's been killed in the bargain."

"Some men could. But not you. You plannin' to say good-bye to Ruth?"

"I'm leaving her to Mr. Cotton," Fargo said. "I know she understands why I had to kill Samuel, but there's no need to go reminding her of it. There's somebody I want you to say good-bye to for me, though."

"Who's that?"

"Silver. I don't think I'll stop by the tent, but you might want to."

"Why'd I want to?"

"She might want to show her gratitude to somebody, and if I'm not around, she might latch onto the next handiest person."

"You think just because I'm old and shot up, missin' an ear and all, that she wouldn't like me if it hadn't been for you?"

Fargo laughed. "You're not missing an ear. Big as your ears are, nobody's even going to know there's a piece missing. And you don't have to worry about Silver. She'd like you because you're so handsome."

"I might go by there," Wiley said. "Just to let her know you've left town."

"And to tell her I said good-bye," Fargo told him. "You remember that."

"I'll remember. If you ever get back up this way, stop by the Trail's End and I'll buy you a drink."

"You can count on that," Fargo said, and then he headed down the trail.

LOOKING FORWARD!

**The following is the opening
section of the next novel in the exciting
Trailsman series from Signet:**

THE TRAILSMAN #256
HIGH COUNTRY HORROR

It had been too long, Skye Fargo thought as he reined the
big black-and-white stallion to a halt. Too long since he
had seen these rugged mountains that loomed before him,
their rocky, snow-capped summits reaching toward the bril-
liantly blue sky above them. Fargo drew in a deep breath
of the clean, crisp, cold air, savoring it. He thought he
smelled snow, but that could have been his imagination
since the sky was clear. He patted the Ovaro's shoulder.
The magnificent horse nickered in a companionable fash-
ion, as if to say that he enjoyed the spectacular view as
much as Fargo did.

But then the lake-blue eyes of the big man in buckskins
narrowed as a frown creased his forehead. Something was
wrong.

Some people said that Skye Fargo had the keenest eye-
sight and the sharpest hearing of any man west of the Mis-
sissippi—and probably east of the Father of Waters, too.
That was why he was the best tracker and trailsman to be
found. Fargo had never really believed that of himself; no
matter how good a man was at anything, there was always
somebody out there somewhere in the world who was bet-

ter. He knew he had good eyes and ears, though. He had to, in order to have lived as long as he had on the frontier. Now those senses told him there was something amiss about the scene before him, and as he leaned forward in the saddle, he realized what it was.

He was on the edge of the Snake River Plain northwest of Fort Hall, one of the stops along the Oregon Trail, the great immigrant trace that led from Independence, Missouri, to the Pacific Northwest. But Fargo was facing north at the moment, looking toward the Sawtooth Mountains and the Lost River Range. The Oregon Trail was behind him. There shouldn't have been any wagon trains in this part of the country, especially not at this time of year. It was late fall, and winter could come crashing down at any time with little or no warning.

Unless he was seeing things, though, those tiny white dots moving into the mountains in the distance were wagons. The bleached canvas covers over the wagon beds stood out sharply against the greens, browns, grays, and blues of the wilderness landscape.

"What in blazes are a bunch of pilgrims doing up here?" Fargo asked the Ovaro. He didn't think there was anything unusual about talking aloud to the horse. The two of them were longtime companions, and the stallion had been a better friend to Fargo than many of the humans he had known. Unfortunately, the horse couldn't answer him in words. The Ovaro tossed his head, however, as if he shared Fargo's concern.

"Yeah," Fargo said. "Reckon we'd better go take a look."

The wagon train was miles away, and even though Fargo knew that he and the stallion could make much better time than those slow-moving prairie schooners, he realized it might be dark before he caught up to them. The emigrants would stop and camp when night fell, but Fargo could continue on. He had no doubt he would be able to locate the wagons. The travelers would build cooking fires, and the sight of the flames and the smell of the smoke would serve as beacons.

Those pilgrims had better hope that he was the only one

drawn to their camp, Fargo thought. The Shoshones had been pretty peaceful of late, but there was no way of knowing when some of the young warriors might take it into their heads to run off some horses for fun. A raid on the wagon train, even a raid that the Indians didn't take completely seriously, could lead to shooting, and that could cause some real problems.

Fargo told himself not to borrow trouble. He put the Ovaro into a ground-eating lope and started making up the distance between the wagons and him.

As he expected, darkness settled over the landscape before he caught up to the wagon train. That slowed him down, because the moon had not yet risen. Fargo could navigate by starlight, but not as well. Tonight, the moon would be almost full. Once it was up, he would be able to increase his pace again.

As he rode, he thought about possible explanations for the odd sight he was on his way to investigate. He supposed that a wagon train could have strayed off the main trail and headed north into the mountains, thinking they were going the right way. That was unlikely, though. Most groups of emigrants hired experienced guides to lead them to what they hoped would be their promised land. Fargo himself had guided more than one wagon train across the frontier. No guide worth his salt could have gotten so turned around, and not many would still be traveling with winter about to come on, unless they knew they were close enough to their destination to risk it.

Maybe there was a new trail he didn't know about. It had been a while since he'd been in this part of the country. It might be the pilgrims in the wagon train were on their way to a new settlement somewhere up yonder in the valley of the Big Lost River. Fargo didn't think that was the case, though. At the head of that valley were some of the tallest, most rugged peaks in these parts. The valley wasn't really good farming or ranching land. This was fur-trapping country, or at least it had been before hordes of mountain men had journeyed to the region back in the thirties and forties and taken most of the beaver plews. Fargo seemed to recall hearing about a trappers' fort being located somewhere in this area, but it had long since been abandoned. Some trapping still went on, but the fur industry wasn't the power it had once been.

No, the more he turned it over in his head, the less reason Fargo could see for those wagons to be heading into the mountains. A feeling of unease began to grow inside him as he climbed to a narrow pass and rode through it into the Big Lost River valley. Out here on the frontier, something that didn't have a good explanation usually had a bad one. He urged the Ovaro into a little faster gait, even though the light still wasn't good.

He had ridden less than a mile when he heard an ominous popping in the distance. The sounds were faint but recognizable.

Gunshots.

"Damn it," Fargo grated. He heeled the stallion into a trot. Even though it was dark, he had to make tracks now. There was trouble up ahead.

But he couldn't help anybody if the horse stumbled and fell and broke a leg or went lame. He would then be afoot and wouldn't be able to reach the wagons for hours. He had to hold the Ovaro back from the breakneck pace the stallion would have adopted if Fargo had given him his head. Fargo had to balance the need to reach his destination safely against the urge to hurry.

The shooting died away after a short time. Fargo bit back another curse. Whatever had happened up there at the emigrant camp, it was over now. Maybe he wouldn't be too late to help. All he could do was hope.

More than an hour after the sun went down, Fargo spotted a good-sized fire up ahead. By now the moon was up, casting silvery illumination over the twisting trail on which Fargo rode. He was already moving fast, but when he saw the fire he let the Ovaro run. The path he had to follow through the winding valley cut him off from sight of the blaze from time to time, but he was always able to find it again. Something big was burning.

He had penetrated miles into the valley before he reached the spot. The Sawtooths rose toweringly to his left, the Lost River Range flanked him on the right. The valley was pretty narrow in most places, with just enough level ground alongside the river for the wagons to travel, but it widened out here and there, and the wagons had come to a stop in one of the wider areas. They had been pulled into a circle with the livestock in the middle, as usual. Fargo estimated the number of wagons at a dozen. One of them was still on fire, and the garish glare from the flames revealed that two more of the vehicles were nothing but burned-out husks. Quite a few people were standing around watching the blaze, not even trying to put out the flames. Fargo guessed they figured the burning wagon was too far gone to save, even though the river was nearby.

Some of the bystanders must have heard the pounding of the Ovaro's hooves over the crackling and popping of the conflagration, because several of them turned toward Fargo. One of them, a man with a bushy black beard, was holding a rifle. To Fargo's surprise, the man jerked the weapon to his shoulder and started drawing a bead on him.

"Don't shoot!" Fargo yelled, but sparks geysered from the barrel of the rifle as the man pulled the trigger. Fargo was already using his knees to swerve the stallion to the side. The move came just in time. He heard the flat *whap!* of the bullet passing by his head, much too close for comfort.

"Hold your fire, damn it!" Fargo shouted again, but he could see that the bearded man was already levering another shell into the rifle's chamber. The weapon was a Henry repeater like the one Fargo carried, and fully loaded it held fifteen rounds. Fargo didn't want to have to shoot the man, but he wasn't going to just let himself be ventilated, either. With a yell, he sent the Ovaro lunging forward in a gallop, straight at the man with the rifle.

The man triggered another shot, but it went wild. Fargo knew that hitting something coming straight at you was one of the most difficult shots to make. The stallion covered the rest of the ground between Fargo and the rifleman as the man was trying to work the weapon's lever. Fargo veered the horse to the side again, kicked his feet free of the stirrups, and left the saddle in a diving tackle that sent him crashing into the rifleman.

The impact of the collision sent the man flying backward off his feet. Fargo landed on top of him, knocking the breath out of the man's lungs. He lay there on the ground, stunned and gasping for air, unable to put up a fight as Fargo jerked the Henry out of his hands and rolled off to the side. Fargo was a little shaken, too, but he didn't allow that to slow him down as he came to his feet and whirled to face the rest of the pilgrims. The rifle was in his hands, ready for use if he needed it. He didn't want to shoot any of these people unless he had to, and even then, he would try to wound, rather than kill.

It took only a second for Fargo to realize that the rest of the crowd represented no threat to him. They were all standing around gaping. Quite a few of them were women and children. Several of the men seemed to be wounded. Fargo saw bloodstains on their clothes and crude bandages wrapped around arms and legs and heads. None of them appeared to be armed. The Henry rifle he was now holding seemed to be the only gun left in the camp.

Fargo raised his voice so that they could hear him over the noise of the burning wagon. "You folks take it easy! I'm here to help you if I can, not to cause more trouble for you."

One of the women took a tentative step forward. "You're not another thief?"

"No, ma'am," Fargo assured her. "I heard the shooting and figured there was trouble up here, so I caught up to you as fast as I could."

"You're a . . . liar!" The choked-out words came from behind Fargo, from the bearded man he had knocked down. "You're . . . one of them!"

Fargo stepped to the side and turned so that he could look down at the man. "One of who?" he asked.

"Those bastards . . . working with Corrigan! Damned thieves!"

"I don't know who Corrigan is," Fargo said. "And I'm not a thief. My name is Fargo. Skye Fargo."

No other series has this much historical action!

THE TRAILSMAN

To order call: 1-800-788-6262

SIGNET BOOKS   (0451)

JUDSON GRAY

RANSOM RIDERS   20418-2

When Penn and McCutcheon are ambushed on
their way to rescue a millionaire's kidnapped
niece, they start to fear that the kidnapping was an
inside job.

CAYWOOD VALLEY FEUD   20656-8

Penn and McCutcheon are back! This third novel
of the American frontier takes readers to the
Ozarks, where a mysterious gunman has been
terrorizing an Ozark family called Caywood—picking them off one by one. The gunman's descrip-
tion matches McCutcheon's good friend Jake Penn.
And now, he must find Penn and prove him
innocent before more blood is spilled.

To order call: 1-800-788-6262